Alex
FEELS THE PINCH

Also by Charles Peattie and Russell Taylor published by Headline

ALEX CALLS THE SHOTS

ALEX PLAYS THE GAME

ALEX KNOWS THE SCORE

ALEX SWEEPS THE BOARD

Alex
FEELS THE PINCH

CHARLES PEATTIE
AND
RUSSELL TAYLOR

HEADLINE

First published in 1997
by HEADLINE BOOK PUBLISHING

10 9 8 7 6 5 4 3 2 1

ISBN 0 7472 7696 X

Printed and bound in Italy by
Canale & C. S.p.A.

HEADLINE BOOK PUBLISHING
A division of Hodder Headline PLC
338 Euston Road
London NW1 3BH

The Telegraph

Alex
PEATTIE + TAYLOR
PRETTY MUCH EVERYONE MANAGED TO STRUGGLE IN ON YESTERDAY'S TRAIN STRIKE DAY. GOOD, CONSIDERING IT WAS SUCH A SWELTERING THURSDAY...
MEGA BANK
AFTER ALL THE UNION LEADERS HAD SUCCEEDED IN MAKING THE PROSPECT OF A LONG TREK INTO WORK MOST UNATTRACTIVE FOR OFFICE WORKERS...
MEGA BANK
GOOD TO KNOW THAT THOSE FEW SCHEMING UNSCRUPULOUS INDIVIDUALS' PLANS TO SABOTAGE THE RUNNING OF OUR BUSINESS WENT ASTRAY...
THEY CERTAINLY DID...
MEGA BANK
CLIVE LEFT THAT JACKET THERE ON WEDNESDAY NIGHT AND DIDN'T BOTHER TO COME IN AT ALL YESTERDAY...
FORGETTING THAT TODAY IS CASUAL DRESS DAY... THAT PINSTRIPE IS A DEAD GIVEAWAY...

Alex
BEATTIE + TAYLOR
HE JUST SITS HERE IN THE OFFICE TILL WELL INTO THE EVENING BUT HE HASN'T REALLY GOT ANY WORK TO DO...
IT'S A COMMON SYNDROME. A HUSBAND INVENTS EXCUSES TO STAY LATE AT THE OFFICE TO AVOID ALL THE TRAUMAS AND HASSLES OF HIS KIDS' BATH- AND BED-TIME
IT REALLY IS SAD AND PATHETIC WHEN A MAN DELIBERATELY DECIDES TO EVADE HIS PARENTAL RESPONSIBILITIES LIKE THAT...
...BUT HE IS MY BOSS AND IT WOULD BE HIGHLY IMPOLITIC OF ME TO LEAVE THE OFFICE BEFORE HIM, DARLING...
YOU RAT... YOU'VE GOT YOUR EXCUSE DOWN TO A TEE HAVEN'T YOU?

BEDTIME STORY BOOK

Alex
PEATTIE + TAYLOR
YOU REALISE WE CAN'T POSSIBLY SUBSTANTIATE THESE ALLEGATIONS OF GROSS FINANCIAL MISMANAGEMENT YOU'RE MAKING AGAINST YOUR ADVERSARIES IN THIS TAKEOVER BATTLE, SIR COLIN?
EH? WHAT?
SO I CALLED IN A JOURNALIST FOR A STRICTLY-OFF-THE-RECORD BRIEFING. HE'LL BE RUNNING THE STORY TOMORROW, PUTTING IT DOWN OF COURSE TO NON-ATTRIBUTABLE SOURCES...
TAP TAP
AH... EXCELLENT WORK, ALEX...
HOLD ON... BUT IF YOU'RE HANDLING THE NEWSPAPERS WHY AM I PAYING A FORTUNE TO A P.R. COMPANY TO BE RESPONSIBLE FOR PRESS LIAISON?
OH, THEY STILL HAVE AN IMPORTANT ROLE TO PLAY, SIR COLIN...
WHICH IS...?
THEY HAVE TO TAKE THE RAP WHEN THE STORY APPEARS...
SPLENDID... WORTH EVERY PENNY...

Alex
PEATTIE + TAYLOR
HARDCASTLE A.G.M.
SO MANY AGMs THESE DAYS USE THESE SECRET COMPUTER SCREENS BUILT INTO THE TABLE WHERE THE DIRECTORS SIT...
AGM
...INVISIBLE TO THE AUDIENCE AND WIRED UP TO A COMPUTER IN AN ADJOINING ROOM WHERE A TEAM OF EXPERTS CAN SILENTLY RELAY INFORMATION THROUGH TO THE DIRECTORS DURING THE MEETING.
JOLLY HANDY WHEN YOU'RE FACING IRATE SHAREHOLDERS...
OF COURSE HARDCASTLE LIKES TO PLAY IT THE OLD-FASHIONED WAY. HE DOESN'T HOLD WITH HAVING A LOAD OF ADVISERS SITTING ANONYMOUSLY IN SOME BACK ROOM HELPING HIM FEND OFF ANY TOUGH QUESTIONS FROM THE FLOOR...
NO INDEED...
HE PREFERS TO HAVE US SITTING ANONYMOUSLY OUT IN THE HALL FEEDING HIM LOTS OF EASY QUESTIONS.
DO YOU WANT TO ASK HIM ABOUT HIS CHARITY WORK OR SHALL I ?
HARDCASTLE AGM
AGM

Alex
PEATTIE + TAYLOR
THE MASS AVAILABILITY OF VIDEO RECORDING TECHNOLOGY HAS CERTAINLY CHANGED THE WAY WE LIVE, BUT NOT NECESSARILY FOR THE BETTER.
SPEAKING PERSONALLY I RESENT THE INTRUSION INTO MY LIFE... CAMERAS EVERYWHERE MAKING RECORDS OF THINGS THAT SHOULD BE ALLOWED TO REMAIN MY OWN PERSONAL BUSINESS AND RESPONSIBILITY...
I COULDN'T AGREE MORE...
IT'S SO EASY FOR THOSE MECHANICAL EYES TO BECOME A TOOL OF THE PEOPLE THAT SEEK TO CONTROL AND MANIPULATE US, ROBBING US OF OUR INDEPENDENCE AND FREEDOM OF ACTION...
MY OLIVER EASILY WON... LOOK...
RUBBISH... MY FOOTAGE CLEARLY SHOWS THAT CHRISTOPHER CROSSED THE LINE FIRST...
HE PUSHED MY TIMOTHY... I'VE GOT IT ON TAPE...
EGG AND SPOON RACE FINISH
RIGHT... THAT'S IT... CAMCORDERS ARE DEFINITELY BANNED FROM NEXT YEAR'S SPORTS DAY...

Alex
PEATTIE + TAYLOR
THINGS WERE THAT TIGHT MONEYWISE FOR SO LONG... IN MY JOB I WAS REALLY UNDER A LOT OF PRESSURE.
YEAH. ME TOO
YOU KNOW WHAT IT'S LIKE... THE STRESS OF HAVING TO SMILE POLITELY AND PUT A BRAVE FACE ON IT WHILE INSIDE YOU'RE BOTTLING UP ALL THIS ANGER AND FRUSTRATION.
VERY HARD...
QUITE HONESTLY I DON'T THINK I COULD'VE BORN THE PRESSURE OF KEEPING UP THAT FRONT FOR MUCH LONGER... THANK GOODNESS THE ECONOMY HAS PICKED UP AT LAST... I FEEL SO MUCH MORE RELAXED NOW...
BECAUSE YOU CAN BE TOTALLY STROPPY AND BOLSHIE WITH ALL YOUR FARES AGAIN?
YEAH... TELLING THEM TO NAFF OFF IF THEY ASK FOR RECEIPTS... REFUSING TO GO SOUTH OF THE RIVER...
TAXI RANK

Alex
PEATTIE + TAYLOR
IT MUST BE DIFFICULT FOR YOU ROMBURGS CHAPS BEING THE ONLY MAJOR BANK IN THE CITY TO HAVE A 5-DAY-A-WEEK CASUAL DRESS POLICY...
HOW DO YOU MEAN?
WELL, PEOPLE IN OUR BUSINESS ARE INTRINSICALLY CONFORMIST, LIKE TO BLEND IN, SHY AWAY FROM INDIVIDUALITY... DON'T YOU FEEL RATHER UNDERDRESSED WHEN YOU MEET OTHER CITY FOLK?
NOT AT ALL, ALEX. I ACTUALLY RELISH THE FACT THAT I'M ATTIRED IN THIS WAY...
OUR CASUAL DRESS BRANDS US AS UNIQUE, DIFFERENT FROM ALL OUR COMPETITORS... IT UNITES US, INSTILS A SENSE OF CORPORATE IDENTITY, ENGENDERS A HEALTHY "US AGAINST THE REST" MENTALITY IN US...
THERE. YOU SEE, CLIVE, IT IS JUST A UNIFORM...
OH. THAT'S ALL RIGHT THEN...

Alex
PEATTIE + TAYLOR
SO, GRIGGS, DO I DETECT THAT YOU'RE A LITTLE UNCOMFORTABLE WITH MY STYLE AS YOUR NEW CHIEF EXEC?
WELL... ER...
MY PREDECESSOR HAD HIS OFFICE UP ON THE 8TH FLOOR WHEREAS I PREFER TO HAVE MINE ON THE TRADING FLOOR ITSELF WITH THIS WINDOW PROVIDING A FULL VIEW OF EVERYTHING THAT GOES ON.
FINDING YOURSELF UNDER OBSERVATION MAKES IT RATHER AWKWARD FOR YOU CHAPS, DOESN'T IT?
WELL... JUST A LITTLE...
ANYWAY... SO WHAT WERE YOU SAYING ABOUT THE UNIQUE CONTRIBUTION YOU ALREADY FELT I'D MADE TO THE COMPANY?
LOOK AT GRIGGS... TONGUE WELL IN THERE.
LITTLE CRAWLER...

TOAD FLAP

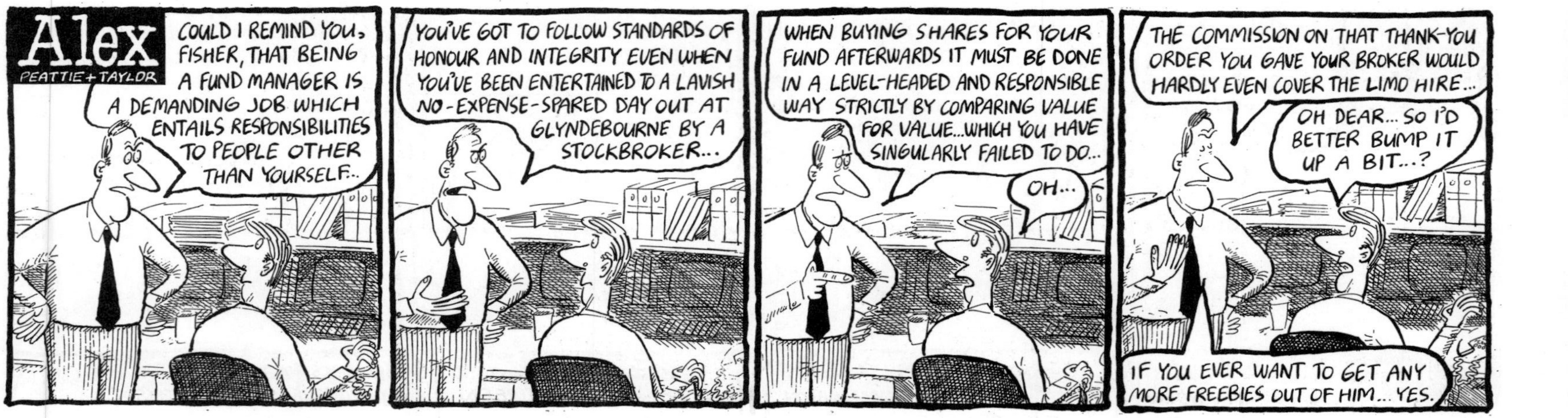
Alex
PEATTIE + TAYLOR
COULD I REMIND YOU, FISHER, THAT BEING A FUND MANAGER IS A DEMANDING JOB WHICH ENTAILS RESPONSIBILITIES TO PEOPLE OTHER THAN YOURSELF...
YOU'VE GOT TO FOLLOW STANDARDS OF HONOUR AND INTEGRITY EVEN WHEN YOU'VE BEEN ENTERTAINED TO A LAVISH NO-EXPENSE-SPARED DAY OUT AT GLYNDEBOURNE BY A STOCKBROKER...
WHEN BUYING SHARES FOR YOUR FUND AFTERWARDS IT MUST BE DONE IN A LEVEL-HEADED AND RESPONSIBLE WAY STRICTLY BY COMPARING VALUE FOR VALUE...WHICH YOU HAVE SINGULARLY FAILED TO DO...
OH...
THE COMMISSION ON THAT THANK-YOU ORDER YOU GAVE YOUR BROKER WOULD HARDLY EVEN COVER THE LIMO HIRE...
OH DEAR... SO I'D BETTER BUMP IT UP A BIT...?
IF YOU EVER WANT TO GET ANY MORE FREEBIES OUT OF HIM... YES.

Alex
PEATTIE + TAYLOR
AND CAN YOU BELIEVE THIS? HE'S STILL BLAMING IT ON THE GOLF COURSE DETERIORATING SINCE LAST SUMMER...
WHOOPS. YOUR MAN'S COME A CROPPER AGAIN...
BLAST.. THERE'S A BLOOMING HUMP HERE!
FOR GOODNESS' SAKE, THE TURF ON THESE GREENS IS TENDED ASSIDUOUSLY BY TEAMS OF SPECIALIST HORTI-CULTURALISTS WHOSE JOB IS TO KEEP THE PLAYING SURFACES IN TIP-TOP CONDITION...
I MEAN, I RECKON IT'S RIDICULOUS TO SUGGEST THAT IN THE LAST YEAR THE GROUND HERE HAS GOT "BUMPIER". WHAT WOULD YOU SAY?
FLATTER IF ANYTHING.
OH YES... GOOD IDEA.
VERY PERCEPTIVE OF YOU, SIR. YES I THINK YOU'RE RIGHT ABOUT THE LUMPS... MY! YOU HAVE GOT A GOOD MEMORY FOR GROUND LIE...
I MEAN, YOU WANT A GOOD TIP, DON'T YOU?

Alex
PEATTIE + TAYLOR
WELL, IT'S THE SILLY SEASON. ZERO GOING ON, EVERYONE ON HOLIDAY AND NEWSPAPERS HAVE GOT NOTHING TO WRITE ABOUT.
YOU'RE TELLING ME.
THE PEOPLE WHO WRITE THIS STUFF REALLY MUST HAVE NO IMAGINATION. DO THEY REALLY THINK THAT THE READER IS NOT GOING TO SEE THROUGH THIS PATHETIC VENEER?
QUITE.
...AS IF WE WERE TOO STUPID TO DISTINGUISH BETWEEN UNREMARKABLE BLAND NOTHINGEY GUFF AND A PROPER MEATY STORY...
BROMEX'S FINANCE DIRECTOR HAS LEFT "TO PURSUE PERSONAL INTERESTS"... SOUNDS LIKE THERE'S BEEN A REAL BOARDROOM BUST-UP THERE...
AND US WITH NOTHING BETTER TO DO THAN TO PROBE INTO IT... BAD LUCK THEM...
DAILY BUGLE CITY OFFICE
PRESS RELEASE

Alex
PEATTIE + TAYLOR
WELL, CLIVE THERE'S NOTHING BETTER THAN AN AFTERNOON AT THE CRICKET...
AND WHAT MORE PICTURESQUE GROUND THAN CANTERBURY?
INDEED SO, CLIVE, BOASTING THAT FAMOUS OLD OAK TREE INSIDE THE BOUNDARY ROPE
THAT'S ALWAYS PUZZLED ME...
...WHY DID THEY BUILD A CRICKET GROUND WITH A TREE ON IT? I MEAN, THEY MUST HAVE REALISED THAT IT WOULD PROVIDE A VISUAL IMPEDIMENT FOR SPECTATORS...
...YET THEY DIDN'T HAVE T.V. COVERAGE BACK THEN.
FORESIGHT, CLIVE... IT'S CERTAINLY USEFUL THESE DAYS FOR AVOIDING BEING SPOTTED BY ONE'S BOSS...

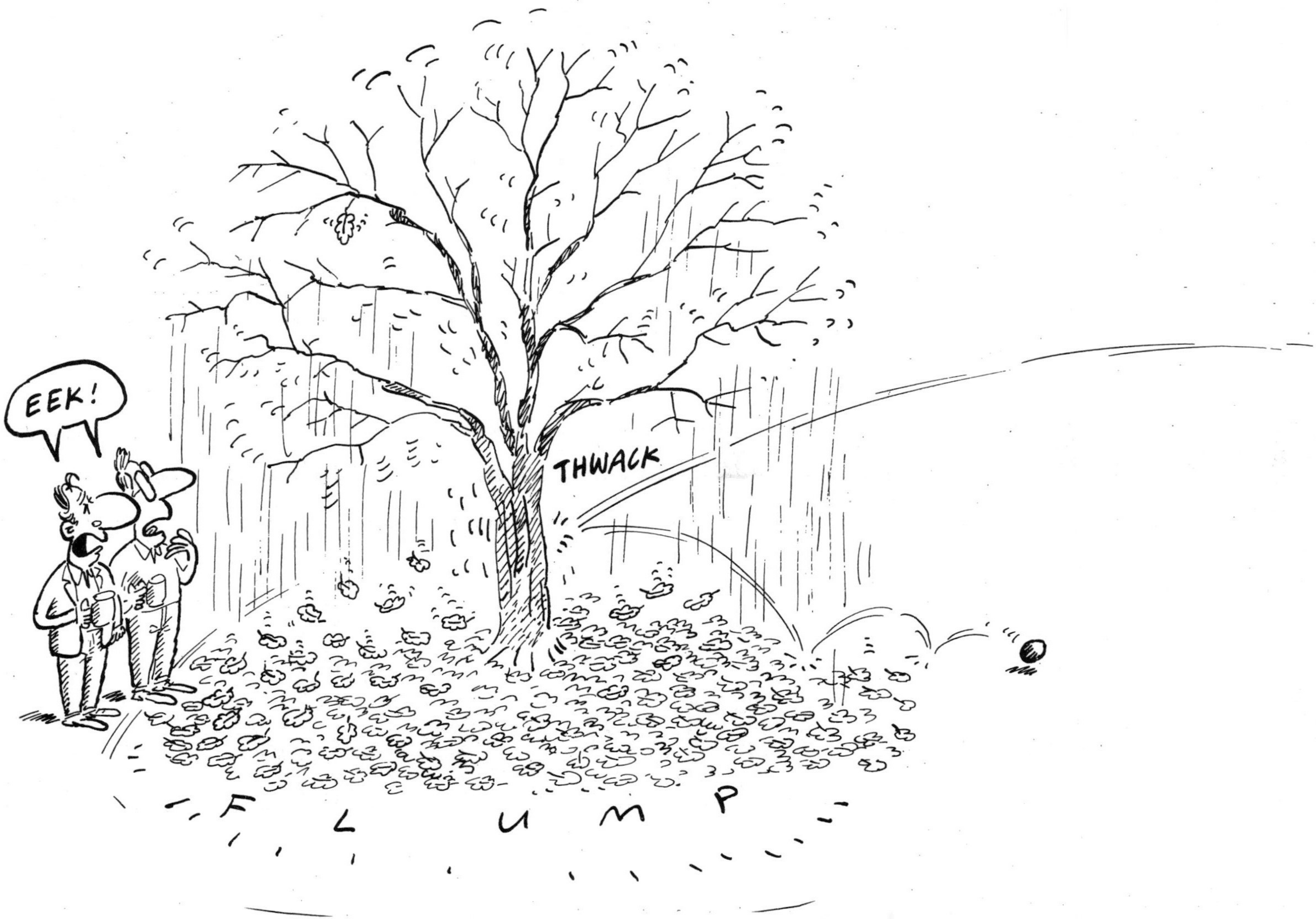
EEK!
THWACK
FLUMP

Alex
PEATTIE + TAYLOR
LOOK AT THAT CHAP DRESSED UP TO THE NINES. WHAT A GRATIFYING SIGHT, EH?
TRADITIONAL EVENING DRESS - THE FORMAL ATTIRE OF THE ENGLISH GENTLEMAN WHEN ATTENDING SOCIETY EVENTS...
SEEING THAT MAN STRIDING DOWN THE STREET, HIS D.J. AND BLACK TIE SIGNALLING TO THE WORLD HIS STATUS, IMPORTANCE AND WORTH IN SOCIETY...
ABSOLUTELY ZERO. IT'S 3 P.M. SO HE MUST BE OFF TO GLYNDEBOURNE... AND IT'S "LULU" TONIGHT...
EXACTLY. ONLY JUNIORS END UP HAVING TO SEE THAT 20TH CENTURY STUFF WITH NO TUNES...
TAXI!

Alex
PEATTIE + TAYLOR
NO QUESTION OF US STAYING AT HOME BECAUSE OF TODAY'S STRIKE.
QUITE. WE'RE OBLIGED TO FIND OUR WAY IN TO WORK SOMEHOW COME WHAT MAY...
IT'S ONLY PEOPLE LIKE OUR CLIENTS WHO HAVE THE OPTION OF CANCELLING LONG-STANDING ARRANGEMENTS WHEN THEY CAN'T FACE THE TRAFFIC DISRUPTION CAUSED BY THE INDUSTRIAL ACTION...
MEANING TODAY I STRUGGLE IN TO WORK AND WHAT DO I FIND? THAT MY CLIENT HAS PHONED IN AT THE LAST MINUTE TO SAY HE'S DECIDED NOT TO MEET ME IN LONDON AFTER ALL...
AND ALL THANKS TO THOSE TRAIN DRIVERS...
MY UTTER TOTAL HEROES! MEANING YOU SUDDENLY HAVE A SPARE TICKET TO LORDS...
YES. FANCY COMING? WE CAN DRINK A TOAST TO ASLEF IN THE COMFORT OF OUR HOSPITALITY BOX...
TEST MATCH

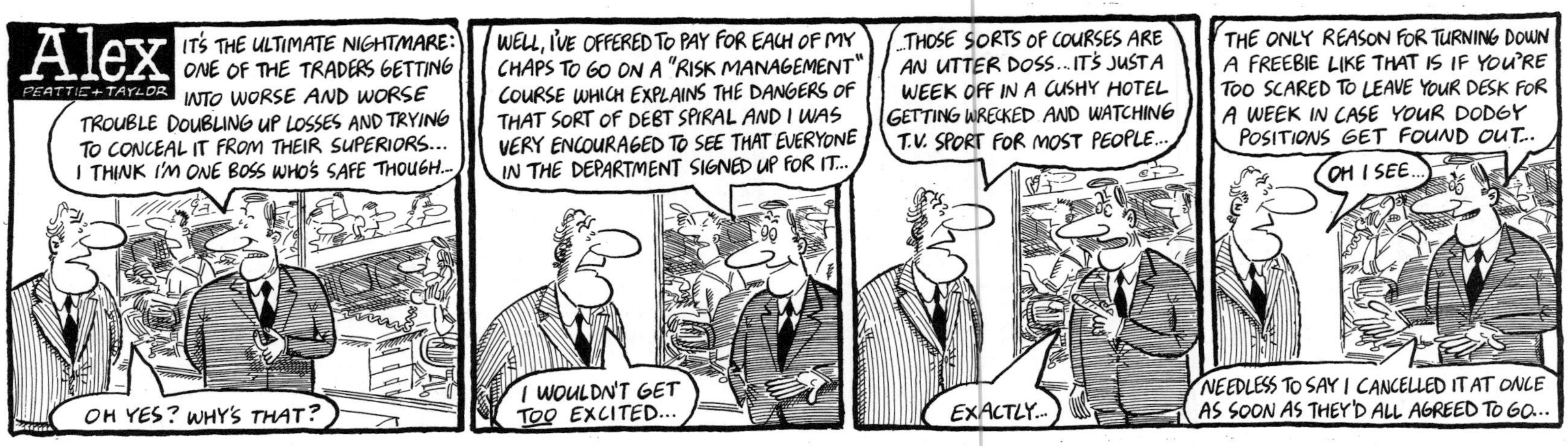
Alex
PEATTIE+TAYLOR
IT'S THE ULTIMATE NIGHTMARE: ONE OF THE TRADERS GETTING INTO WORSE AND WORSE TROUBLE DOUBLING UP LOSSES AND TRYING TO CONCEAL IT FROM THEIR SUPERIORS... I THINK I'M ONE BOSS WHO'S SAFE THOUGH...
OH YES? WHY'S THAT?
WELL, I'VE OFFERED TO PAY FOR EACH OF MY CHAPS TO GO ON A "RISK MANAGEMENT" COURSE WHICH EXPLAINS THE DANGERS OF THAT SORT OF DEBT SPIRAL AND I WAS VERY ENCOURAGED TO SEE THAT EVERYONE IN THE DEPARTMENT SIGNED UP FOR IT...
I WOULDN'T GET TOO EXCITED...
...THOSE SORTS OF COURSES ARE AN UTTER DOSS... IT'S JUST A WEEK OFF IN A CUSHY HOTEL GETTING WRECKED AND WATCHING T.V. SPORT FOR MOST PEOPLE...
EXACTLY...
THE ONLY REASON FOR TURNING DOWN A FREEBIE LIKE THAT IS IF YOU'RE TOO SCARED TO LEAVE YOUR DESK FOR A WEEK IN CASE YOUR DODGY POSITIONS GET FOUND OUT...
OH I SEE...
NEEDLESS TO SAY I CANCELLED IT AT ONCE AS SOON AS THEY'D ALL AGREED TO GO...

Alex
PEATTIE + TAYLOR
AS A LIFETIME NON-SMOKER, OBVIOUSLY I'M GLAD FOR HEALTH REASONS THAT THIS ORGANISATION HAS A SMOKING BAN.
OF COURSE
SO I GUESS YOU MUST HAVE STRONG VIEWS ON THE FACT THAT BY VIRTUE OF HIS POSITION OUR BOSS IS ABLE TO SMOKE IN HIS OFFICE...
I CERTAINLY DO.
AT MY LAST COMPANY THE SMOKING BAN WAS STRICTLY ENFORCED AND IF THE BOSS WANTED TO LIGHT UP HE HAD TO JOIN THE GAGGLE OF OTHER NICOTINE ADDICTS OUTSIDE THE BUILDING...
THAT MUST HAVE MADE A BIG DIFFERENCE PSYCHOLOGICALLY...
YES...
... I WAS TOTALLY PARANOID... ESPECIALLY JUST BEFORE BONUS TIME, SEEING ALL THOSE BROWN-NOSING SMOKERS GETTING A CHANCE TO BUTTON-HOLE HIM IN PRIVATE...
LONG MAY RUPERT CONTINUE TO FLOUT THE RULES, EH?

Alex
BEATTIE + TAYLOR
I'M SUPPOSED TO GO ON HOLIDAY TOMORROW...BUT THERE ARE LOOSE ENDS ON THIS DEAL THAT NEED TYING UP... NOTHING TOO IMPORTANT, BUT I SUPPOSE I COULD ALWAYS FLY OUT AND JOIN MY FAMILY LATER...
ANDREW WHAT ARE YOU BEATING YOURSELF UP FOR? JUST THINK, ARE YOU REALLY NEEDED? ARE YOU NOT JUST FEELING GUILTY ABOUT TASKS WHICH COULD EQUALLY WELL BE PERFORMED BY SOMEONE ELSE IN YOUR ABSENCE?
WELL... I SUPPOSE...
RIGHT NOW YOU NEED RELAXATION NOT MORE STRESS AND FRUSTRATION SO STOP WORRYING ABOUT DUMPING ON OTHERS AND JUST THINK OF YOURSELF, OKAY?
THANKS, ALEX, YOU'RE RIGHT OF COURSE...
SO I STAY HERE AND SHUFFLE PAPERS FOR A DAY OR TWO..?
YES, AND FLY OUT AND JOIN YOUR FAMILY ONCE YOUR WIFE'S HAD THE HASSLE OF TAKING THE KIDS ON THE PLANE, GETTING THEM TO THE VILLA ETC ETC...

Alex
PEATTIE + TAYLOR
WHAT'S WRONG, CHRISTOPHER?
IT'S DADDY. I JUST KNOW WHEN HE COMES DOWN HE'S GOING TO WANT TO PLAY THAT STUPID GAME WITH ME...
HE REALLY TREATS ME LIKE AN IDIOT. I MEAN I'M SEVEN YEARS OLD. HIS GUESSING GAMES ARE TOO EASY AND PREDICTABLE...
AH, CHRISTOPHER.
LET'S HAVE A LITTLE GAME OF I-SPY, SHALL WE?... LET'S SEE... I SPY WITH MY LITTLE EYE SOMETHING BEGINNING WITH "P"....
THE REGISTRATION PLATE ON YOUR NEW COMPANY CAR, DADDY...
AH, EXCELLENT.. YOU NOTICED...
WELL THAT'S THAT OVER FOR ANOTHER YEAR...

Alex
PEATTIE + TAYLOR
YOU KNOW, THERE HAVE BEEN SOME SERIOUS SUGGESTIONS FROM TOP LAW OFFICIALS THAT BROTHELS SHOULD BE LEGALISED...
WHAT, JUST GIVEN A LICENCE?
YES... THE ARGUMENTS ARE THAT FROM A HEALTH AND SAFETY POINT OF VIEW IT WOULD MAKE SENSE IF SUCH SERVICES COULD OPERATE AWAY FROM THE STREET INSIDE A LEGITIMATE PLACE OF BUSINESS...
HMMM...
...ONE WOULDN'T WANT TO SEE THAT SORT OF THING GO TOO FAR THOUGH WOULD ONE?
NO, NO... OBVIOUSLY THERE WOULD STILL HAVE TO BE CURBS...
EXACTLY...
I MEAN, CRAWLING ALONG IN THE MOTOR AT 3 M.P.H. IS HALF THE FUN ISN'T IT?

Alex
PEATTIE + TAYLOR
AH, RICHARD. GOOD HOLIDAY?
WONDERFUL, THANKS, ALEX. ANY OF MY CLIENTS PHONE WHILST I WAS AWAY?
HEALTHY GLOW
YES, BUT NOTHING WE COULDN'T HANDLE. I'M GLAD TO SAY THE "HOLIDAY NOTES" YOU LEFT DETAILING THE STATE OF PROGRESS OF ALL YOUR DEALS WERE CLEAR AND COMPREHENSIVE...
HOLIDAY NOTES
IN FACT EVERYTHING WENT SWIMMINGLY. YOUR CLIENTS WERE TOTALLY HAPPY, RUPERT WAS KEPT INFORMED AT ALL STAGES AND NO-ONE IN THE DEPARTMENT WAS PUT OUT AT ALL...
OH. THANKS.
YOU REALLY PUT THE WIND UP HIM THERE. NO-ONE LIKES TO FEEL HE'S DISPENSABLE...
TOTAL FUNK
IDIOT. HE SHOULD LEAVE DELIBERATELY VAGUE AND INCOMPLETE NOTES LIKE THE REST OF US..

Alex
BEATTIE + TAYLOR
WHAT ARE YOU DOING, ALEX?
WHAT I ALWAYS DO ONCE WORK ON A DEAL IS COMPLETED AND IT'S BEEN ANNOUNCED.
I'M GETTING ON MY COMPUTER TERMINAL AND SENDING AN E-MAIL MESSAGE OF CONGRATULATIONS TO ALL THE DIFFERENT PEOPLE INVOLVED IN THE SUCCESSFUL OUTCOME... IT'S ABOUT GENERATING A FEELING OF TEAM FELLOWSHIP.
OH.
ATTENTION TO DETAIL IS VERY IMPORTANT AT TIMES LIKE THIS. A LITTLE PERSONAL MEMO EXPRESSING ONE'S APPRECIATION OF AND REGARD FOR EVERYONE'S CONTRIBUTION CAN WORK WONDERS TO GROUP PSYCHOLOGY.
WHAT, LEAVING AN IMPRESSION THAT THE SENDER WAS INVOLVED IN THE DEAL IN SOME WAY? WHICH YOU WEREN'T.
YUP. GOTTA LAY DOWN THE GROUNDWORK FOR STAKING A CLAIM TO A SHARE OF THE BONUS LATER.

Alex
BEATTIE + TAYLOR
CALL ME OLD-FASHIONED BUT I'M GLAD THE TREND FOR BIG BANK TAKE-OVERS FROM ABROAD HAS ENDED...
AFTER ALL BANKING IS A PEOPLE BUSINESS... YOU KNOW WHAT HAPPENS WHEN ENTIRE WORKFORCES ALL JUST GET MERGED INTO THESE BIG AMORPHOUS IMPERSONAL ORGANISATIONS.
I HATED THE WAY ALL THOSE FOREIGN BANKS DESTROYED ALL THE OLD INDIGENOUS SMALLER INSTITUTIONS BY TAKING THEM OVER LOCK, STOCK AND BARREL...
YES, ME TOO...
...WE GOT NO FEES FOR IT DID WE...?
EXACTLY. THANK GOODNESS THEY'VE GONE BACK TO DESTROYING THE COMPETITION BY POACHING ESSENTIAL PERSONNEL INSTEAD...
& HERBERT :-
EXECUTIVE RECRUITMENT CONSULTANTS
LET'S SEE... KRAUTZER BANK WANT AN ENTIRE DERIVATIVES DESK...

Alex
PEATTIE + TAYLOR
SO FOR OUR MEETING IN PARIS TOMORROW - WHAT'S IT TO BE? THE TRAIN OR THE PLANE?
NO-ONE TAKES THE EUROSTAR, CLIVE.
THAT'S TRUE. IT'S RUNNING WAY BELOW CAPACITY I HEAR...
HARDLY SURPRISING. FOR A START THEY DON'T OFFER YOU ANY DECENT PERKS LIKE AIR MILES.
SECONDLY IT'S ACTUALLY QUICKER TO TAKE A FLIGHT FROM CITY AIRPORT TO ORLY...SO FOR PEOPLE LIKE US WHO DON'T WANT TO WASTE ANY TIME ON THEIR TRIP...
THE CHOICE IS CLEAR.
EUROSTAR
EXCELLENT. ONE CAN DISCUSS BUSINESS WITHOUT FEAR OF BEING OVERHEARD.
IT'LL BE A REAL NUISANCE IF THIS THING EVER GETS POPULAR.

MORNING, ALEX..
EUROSTAR 1ST CLASS
1ST CLASS
SHHH...
1ST CLASS

Alex
PEATTIE + TAYLOR
OH HELLO, CLAIRE... SO WHAT'S THE BOSS'S SECRETARY PHONING ME ABOUT...?
OH JUST A CHAT... KENNETH HAS JUST POPPED OUT TO TALK TO SOMEONE IN YOUR OFFICE...
OOH DEAR... DOES THIS MEAN SOMEBODY IS FOR THE CHOP? IS SOMEONE GETTING THE DREADED TAP ON THE SHOULDER AND GRIM-FACED INVITATION TO JOIN KENNETH IN HIS OFFICE?
WELL... SORT OF...
POOR OLD KENNETH! I KNOW WHAT A SENSITIVE SOUL HE IS UNDERNEATH ALL THAT... HOW MUCH HE HATES HAVING TO COME OUT AND ISSUE THOSE SUMMONSES IN PERSON... SO WHO'S GETTING SACKED THIS TIME?
WELL, YOU ACTUALLY... HE JUST ASKED ME TO KEEP YOU TALKING SO HE COULD ASK THE BLOKE NEXT TO YOU TO ASK YOU TO COME AND SEE HIM WHEN YOU GOT OFF THE TELEPHONE...
EEK!
SURE... I'LL TELL HIM...
THANKS.

Alex
PEATTIE + TAYLOR
WHAT'S ALL THIS ABOUT HARDCASTLE & CO SPLITTING IN TWO?
OH DEMERGERS ARE VERY FASHIONABLE IN THE CITY NOW, CLIVE. THIS IS WHERE THE FUTURE IS...
THE TREND FOR BUILDING THESE HUGE DIVERSIFIED CORPORATIONS RUN BY OVERPAID FATCATS UNNACCOUNTABLE TO ANYONE HAS GONE ABOUT AS FAR AS IT CAN... I THINK THE TIDE IS ABOUT TO TURN...
...AND WE'RE FINALLY ABOUT TO SEE AGAIN A RELEASE OF THE ENTREPRENEURIAL INVENTIVE SPIRIT WITHOUT WHICH WEALTH CREATION WOULD BE IMPOSSIBLE.
OH.
RIGHT, LET'S SEE... CHAIRMAN OF TWO COMPANIES SO THAT'S TWO SALARIES FOR YOU...
2 CLIENTS FOR YOU, SO DOUBLE YOUR BANK'S RETAINER...
AND TWICE THE SHARE OPTIONS OF COURSE...
PROD PROD
PROD PROD
PROD
PLUS ALL THE FEES FOR DOING THIS WORK...

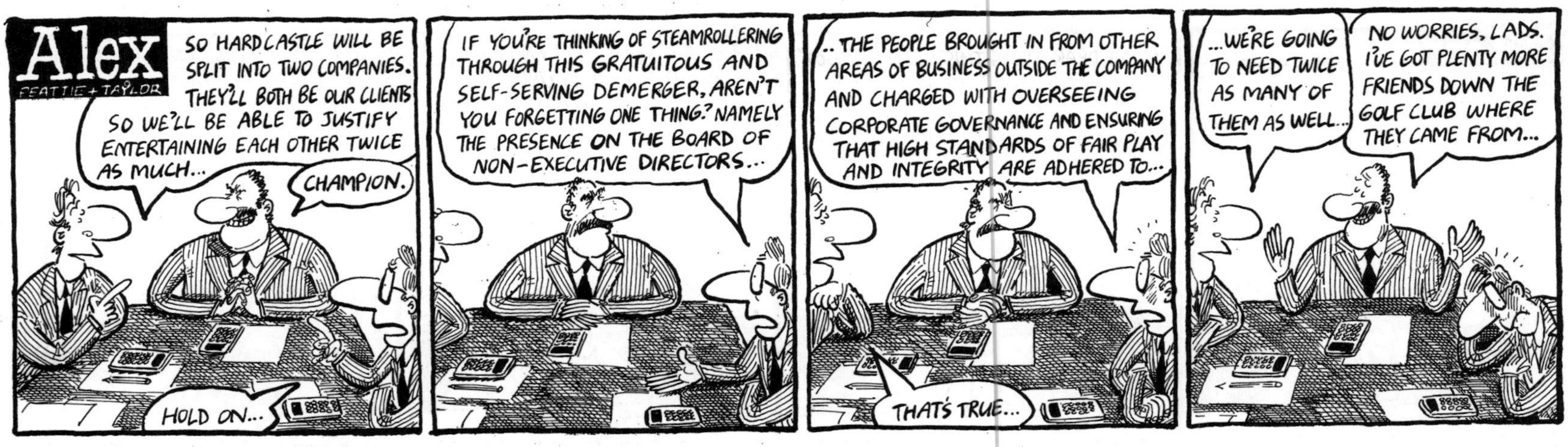
Alex
PEATTIE + TAYLOR
SO HARDCASTLE WILL BE SPLIT INTO TWO COMPANIES. THEY'LL BOTH BE OUR CLIENTS SO WE'LL BE ABLE TO JUSTIFY ENTERTAINING EACH OTHER TWICE AS MUCH...
CHAMPION.
HOLD ON...
IF YOU'RE THINKING OF STEAMROLLERING THROUGH THIS GRATUITOUS AND SELF-SERVING DEMERGER, AREN'T YOU FORGETTING ONE THING? NAMELY THE PRESENCE ON THE BOARD OF NON-EXECUTIVE DIRECTORS...
.. THE PEOPLE BROUGHT IN FROM OTHER AREAS OF BUSINESS OUTSIDE THE COMPANY AND CHARGED WITH OVERSEEING CORPORATE GOVERNANCE AND ENSURING THAT HIGH STANDARDS OF FAIR PLAY AND INTEGRITY ARE ADHERED TO...
THAT'S TRUE...
...WE'RE GOING TO NEED TWICE AS MANY OF THEM AS WELL...
NO WORRIES, LADS. I'VE GOT PLENTY MORE FRIENDS DOWN THE GOLF CLUB WHERE THEY CAME FROM...

Alex
BEATTIE + TAYLOR
WELL, BAKER, AS A TRAINEE DEVELOPING A NOUS FOR THE IMPLICATIONS IN THE FINANCIAL NEWS, HOW'S IT GOING?
INTERESTING ACTUALLY... THERE CERTAINLY SEEMS TO BE A "FEELGOOD" THEME TO A LOT OF BRITISH BUSINESS STORIES AT THE MOMENT...
REALLY?
FINANCIAL
NOTHING TOO SPECIFIC... JUST A GENERALISED TREND OF COMPANIES SOUNDING OPTIMISTIC... MORE NEWS OF EXPANSIONS OR SUCCESSES... THE FUTURE LOOKING A BIT ROSIER...
IS THAT SO?
I MEAN, ONE SIMPLY WASN'T SEEING STORIES LIKE THIS IN THE PAPERS SIX MONTHS AGO WAS ONE?
I DON'T THINK SO, NO.
THOSE SAME STORIES WOULD BE PUT STRAIGHT IN THE BIN BY ANY SELF-RESPECTING JOURNALIST IN MARCH.
SO THIS MUST BE THE "SILLY SEASON" WHEN THEY'LL PRINT ANY OLD RUBBISH THE P.R. JOHNNIES CHOOSE TO SEND THEM?
PAT PAT
GOOD. YOU'RE LEARNING...

Alex
PEATTIE + TAYLOR
WHO WAS THAT ON THE PHONE, DARLING?
IT WAS ONE OF THE CHAPS FROM MY OFFICE - ALEX MASTERLEY...
WHAT? HOW DID HE FIND YOU? I THOUGHT YOU SAID YOU LEFT A DELIBERATELY JUMBLED-UP HOLIDAY CONTACT NUMBER?
I DID. BUT ALEX TRACKED ME DOWN THROUGH INTERNATIONAL DIRECTORY ENQUIRIES... DAMN HIM...
HE WANTED TO TELL ME ABOUT SOME IMPORTANT DEVELOPMENTS OVER IN LONDON...
OH NO, DARLING... I CAN SEE YOU'RE ALL TENSE AND PREOCCUPIED ALREADY... WHAT WAS IT?
APPARENTLY THERE ARE TUBE STRIKES THE DAY BEFORE AND AFTER THE BANK HOLIDAY WEEKEND... EVERYONE IS ON A BONA-FIDE 5-DAY SKIVE BACK THERE... BLAST! I CHOSE THE WRONG FORTNIGHT TO TAKE MY HOLIDAY...
GRRR...

Alex
BEATTIE + TAYLOR
SORRY, ANNA, I CAN'T LEAVE THE OFFICE YET BECAUSE MY HEAD OF DEPARTMENT IS STILL HERE WORKING..
SO IT'S THE USUAL ROUTINE OF YOU GOING TO BE LATE HOME?
YOU KNOW I REALLY RESENT THIS PROTOCOL THAT WHEN BOSSES CAN'T UNWIND AND RELAX YET, THEN THEIR EMPLOYEES HAVE TO SUFFER ALONG WITH THEM PUTTING IN LONG HOURS TOO...
LOOK I'M SORRY BUT...
ALL YOU'RE DOING IS CREATING A FACADE OF BEING CONSCIENTIOUS OUT OF A SENSE OF GUILT AND DUTY THAT DOESN'T REALLY BENEFIT ANYONE YOU KNOW....
WHY CAN'T YOU SAY GOODNIGHT TO YOUR KIDS ON THE PHONE LIKE OTHER WORKING MUMS DO?
LOOK YOU'RE MY NANNY, ANNA, AND IT'S YOUR JOB TO KEEP THEM UP UNTIL I GET HOME...
BUT THEY WANT TO GO TO BED... IT'S NOT FAIR... I'M TIRED...

Alex
BEATTIE + TAYLOR
I'M A BIT WORRIED ABOUT CHRISTOPHER'S SCHOOL, ALEX. THEY HAVE A "PAPERLESS CLASSROOM" APPROACH... HE'S NOT EVEN LEARNING TO WRITE...
THAT'S RATHER SHORT-SIGHTED OF YOU, PENNY... AN EMPHASIS ON WORK PRODUCED ON KEYPAD AND COMPUTER IS ONLY WHAT ONE WOULD EXPECT FROM A TOP PREP SCHOOL LIKE ST CRISPIN'S.
I'D CALL IT HIGHLY ENLIGHTENED THAT ITS PUPILS SHOULD BE TAUGHT THE SKILLS APPROPRIATE TO THEIR EXPECTATIONS OF THE WORLD OF WORK THEY'LL BE GOING INTO IN THEIR ADULT LIVES...
HOMEWORK: THURSDAY... "WHAT I DID IN MY HOLIDAYS" BY CHRISTOPHER MASTERLEY... ER...
OH, AND DON'T FORGET TO PUT THE DISC IN MY SATCHEL, MUMMY...
PRIDE
TYPE TYPE
PACE
PACE
NO, DEAR

Alex
BEATTIE + TAYLOR
I DON'T BELIEVE IT! ARE YOU USING A MOBILE PHONE IN CLASS, MASTERLEY...? WHAT DO YOU THINK YOU'RE DOING?
ER, TRADING CONKER FUTURES, SIR...
DO YOU REALISE HOW MUCH MONEY YOUR PARENTS SPEND TO HAVE YOU EDUCATED HERE, BOY? AND YOU'RE DOING THAT DURING LESSONS... DESIST!
YES, SIR.
NEXT TIME I SHALL GIVE YOU LINES, BOY.
YES, SIR.
BASICALLY I NEED A FAX LINE... A MAIN LAND-LINE ... A PRIVATE LINE... PLUS ONE ON A MODEM FOR MY E-MAIL ORDERS...

Alex
PEATTIE + TAYLOR
ALEX IS COMING TO THE HARDCASTLE MEETING? BUT I THOUGHT HE WAS IN THE STATES FOR A SERIES OF CLIENT VISITS...
HE IS...
BUT HE'S FLYING OVER SPECIALLY ON CONCORDE. HE'LL HAVE TO FLY BACK OUT TO NEW YORK TOMORROW...
WELL, IN HIS PLACE I THINK I'D JUST BOOK MYSELF INTO A HOTEL IN MANHATTAN AND TAKE THE DAY OFF...
I TEND TO AGREE... WHICH IS WHY I ADMIRE ALEX. SEE HOW HE REACTS WHEN THERE'S THE POSSIBILITY OF PLACING HIS OWN INTERESTS BEFORE THOSE OF THE BANK AND OF THINKING ONLY OF HIS OWN PLEASURE AND RELAXATION...
YES...
HE GOES FOR IT WITHOUT A SECOND THOUGHT...
QUITE. WITH ALL THE AIR MILES HE'LL CLOCK UP ON THIS TOTALLY GRATUITOUS ROUND TRIP HE'LL BE ABLE TO TAKE HIS FAMILY TO KLOSTERS FOR XMAS...

Alex
PEATTIE + TAYLOR
WELL, AFTER A YEAR AT MEGABANK BEING A LOWLY GRADUATE TRAINEE THIS IS MY CHANCE TO GET OUT AND DO SOMETHING USEFUL AND PROVE MYSELF...
WHAT IS?
ITS THE TIME OF YEAR WHEN ALL THE BANKS GO AND GIVE THEIR OXBRIDGE CAREER PRESENTATIONS AND THEY TAKE THEIR RECENT RECRUITS LIKE ME ALONG TO GIVE TALKS TO THE UNDERGRADUATES THERE.
OH REALLY?
YES, YOU SEE WORD-OF-MOUTH PERSONAL CONTACT REALLY MAKES A DIFFERENCE THERE... THE IDEA IS THAT I'LL MEET A LOT OF PEOPLE WHO MIGHT HAVE KNOWN ME WHEN I WAS STILL A STUDENT AND I'LL BE ABLE TO TALK TO THEM PERSUASIVELY ABOUT EMPLOYMENT OPPORTUNITIES.
AH YES... THE STUDENTS WHO WERE IN THE YEARS BELOW YOU?
ER... NO... THE ONES IN MY YEAR WHO WENT TO OTHER BANKS... THIS IS MY CHANCE TO NETWORK MYSELF ANOTHER JOB AWAY FROM THESE B*ST*RDS...
NICHOLS... ANOTHER SANDWICH PLEASE?
SCHED-ULE
NOW I WONDER WHEN MINERAL BANK'S PRESENTATION IS?

Alex
BEATTIE + TAYLOR
RUPERT! SO I HEAR YOU'VE BEEN SECONDED TO THE WORLD BANK IN WASHINGTON?
YES. IT'S TO WORK AS AN ADVISOR TO EMERGING ECONOMIES AROUND THE WORLD...
AFTER ALL, THE GREAT PRIVATISATION EXPERIMENT SEEMS TO BE OVER IN THIS COUNTRY... THE CONSERVATIVE PARTY IS TEARING ITSELF APART OVER A "LITTLE ENGLAND" FANTASY OF ISOLATIONISM...
LIFT
BUT THERE ARE OTHER COUNTRIES ABROAD WHOSE SITUATION ECONOMICALLY AND POLITICALLY MAKE THEM HIGHLY RELEVANT TO CERTAIN AREAS OF MY FINANCIAL EXPERTISE.
OF COURSE...
PING
SUCH AS TAX AVOIDANCE YOU MEAN?
QUITE. 2 YEARS IN THE STATES WHEN A NEW LABOUR GOVERNMENT IS SQUEEZING THE FAT CATS OVER HERE. PERFECT.

Alex
PEATTIE + TAYLOR
REMEMBER WHEN WE WERE STILL AT UNIVERSITY AND PEOPLE WHO'D LEFT WOULD COME BACK AND GIVE CAREER PRESENTATIONS FROM THE CITY..?
PEOPLE LIKE NICHOLS, YES.
MEGA-BANK PRESENTATION
WITH THEIR FLASH SUITS AND EXECUTIVE ACCESSORIES AND THEIR TALK OF DEALS AND MEGA-BUCKS... IT MADE ONE SO EAGER TO GET OUT INTO THE OUTSIDE WORLD...
YES... SIGH
ONE DOESN'T REALISE IT AS A STUDENT, DOES ONE? THAT FOR A LOT OF PEOPLE WHO GO ON INTO THE CITY THEIR TIME SPENT HERE WILL HAVE BEEN THE HAPPIEST DAYS OF THEIR LIVES...
THAT'S RIGHT.
THEY'RE THE ONLY COUPLE OF DAYS IN THE YEAR WHEN A GRADUATE TRAINEE CAN GET ANY RESPECT FROM ANYONE, BASICALLY...
COCKY LITTLE RUNT.. WELL IT'S BACK TO FETCHING OUR SANDWICHES AND DRY CLEANING ON MONDAY... HEH HEH HEH...

Alex
PEATTIE + TAYLOR
REMEMBER THE OLD DAYS WHEN WE'D SUBJECT OUR GRADUATE TRAINEES TO MENIAL TASKS AND SILLY PRANKS ABOUT MADE-UP COMPANIES...?
IT WOULD BE A WASTE OF TIME NOW. THEY'RE ALL FAR TOO SUSSED...
YES. THESE DAYS THEY'RE ALL COMPUTER-LITERATE BUSINESS STUDIES GRADUATES. THEY HAVE COMPLETELY DIFFERENT EXPECTATIONS MORE SUITED TO THE COMPETITIVE HI-TECH ENVIRONMENT REPRESENTED BY THE FINANCIAL WORLD...
THESE KIDS HAVE GROWN UP IN THE ERA OF THE MICROCHIP AND THEY'RE USED TO ADAPTING TO ALL THE LATEST TECHNOLOGICAL ADVANCES ... WE IN THE CITY SHOULD BE TAKING ADVANTAGE OF THIS.
YES.
LIKE YOU TELLING LOVETT THAT WE'VE GOT A VOICE-ACTIVATED PHOTOCOPIER...
QUITE.
3 COPIES PLEASE... PRINT.... PRINT!
HEM HEM... A BIT LOUDER, LOVETT... IT'LL WORK IN A MINUTE...

Alex
PEATTIE + TAYLOR
ALEX, OUR NEW HEAD OF DEPARTMENT HAS ARRIVED AND IT'S GRAVE NEWS...
WHAT'S HAPPENED TO ALICE, RUPERT'S OLD SECRETARY?
SHE GOT THE SACK. I'M AFRAID OUR NEW BOSS IS OF THE OPINION THAT FEMALE CLERICAL STAFF SHOULD BE YOUNG, LONG-LEGGED, SHORT-SKIRTED DIM-WITTED BIMBOS...
HEAD OF DEPT.
AND THAT IT IS UNHELPFUL TO OFFICE MORALE TO HAVE SOBERLY-DRESSED MIDDLE-AGED WOMEN WORKING AS SECRETARIES...
HEAD OF DEPT
WHAT? THIS IS OUTRAGEOUS... WHY?
...BECAUSE I DON'T EVER WANT TO GET MISTAKEN FOR ONE...
ALEX, THIS IS OUR NEW BOSS... JANE.
EGAD!

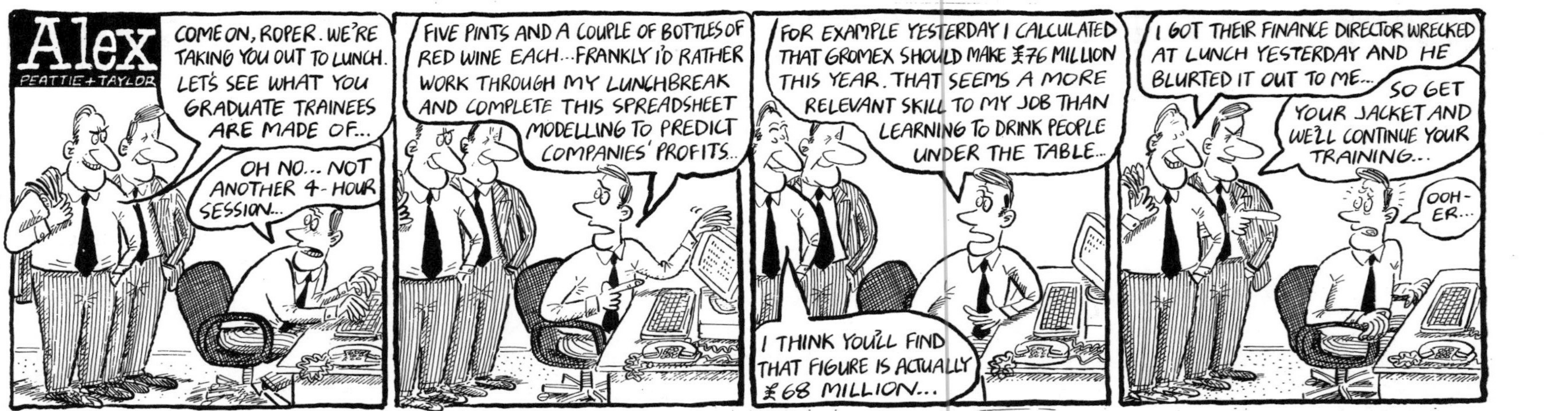
Alex
PEATTIE + TAYLOR
COME ON, ROPER. WE'RE TAKING YOU OUT TO LUNCH. LET'S SEE WHAT YOU GRADUATE TRAINEES ARE MADE OF...
OH NO... NOT ANOTHER 4-HOUR SESSION...
FIVE PINTS AND A COUPLE OF BOTTLES OF RED WINE EACH... FRANKLY I'D RATHER WORK THROUGH MY LUNCHBREAK AND COMPLETE THIS SPREADSHEET MODELLING TO PREDICT COMPANIES' PROFITS...
FOR EXAMPLE YESTERDAY I CALCULATED THAT GROMEX SHOULD MAKE ¥76 MILLION THIS YEAR. THAT SEEMS A MORE RELEVANT SKILL TO MY JOB THAN LEARNING TO DRINK PEOPLE UNDER THE TABLE...
I THINK YOU'LL FIND THAT FIGURE IS ACTUALLY ¥68 MILLION...
I GOT THEIR FINANCE DIRECTOR WRECKED AT LUNCH YESTERDAY AND HE BLURTED IT OUT TO ME...
SO GET YOUR JACKET AND WE'LL CONTINUE YOUR TRAINING...
OOH-ER...

CHAIRMAN
CHIEF EXEC
FINANCE DIRECTOR.

Alex
BEATTIE + TAYLOR
SO WHAT'S THE INITIAL MOOD IN YOUR NEW DEPARTMENT, JANE?
OH MY STAFF WANT TO TEST THE METTLE OF THEIR NEW BOSS, SHOW ME THEY CAN'T BE PUSHED AROUND...
THEY'RE ALL TAKING ANY OPPORTUNITY TO PUT ON A SYMBOLIC SHOW OF DEFIANCE AND STRESS THEIR INDEPENDENCE AND REBELLIOUSNESS...
ESPECIALLY AS TODAY IS CASUAL DRESS DAY WHEN PEOPLE CAN LET THEIR HAIR DOWN AND COME INTO THE OFFICE IN ANY CLOTHES THEY PLEASE...
RIGHT...
SO THEY'RE ALL WEARING THEIR NORMAL SUITS TO HINT THAT THEY MIGHT HAVE A JOB INTERVIEW..?
YAWN YES... I SHALL EXPECT A FEW PETULANT RESIGNATION THREATS IN THE RUN UP TO BONUS TIME...

Alex
BEATTIE + TAYLOR
I WANT TO TALK TO YOU ABOUT YOUR EXPENSES FOR THAT DAY IN FRANKFURT ON BUSINESS LAST MONTH... THIS BILL IS EXCESSIVE...
OH...
THE SWAPS MARKET IS VERY TIGHT AT THE MOMENT AND WE'VE GOT TO KEEP A TIGHT REIN ON EXPENDITURE... NOW, OBVIOUSLY IF YOU'RE GOING TO GET BUSINESS OUT OF GERMAN CLIENTS A CERTAIN AMOUNT OF ENTERTAINING WILL BE NECESSARY...
BUT TRY TO SHOW SOME SENSE AND RESTRAINT AND NOT THROW AWAY HUNDREDS OF POUNDS OF THE BANK'S MONEY ON NEEDLESS WASTEFUL SELF-INDULGENT ITEMS LIKE THIS...
TAP
THE JEROBOAM OF KRUG? THE MAGNUM OF AMAGNAC? THE LAP DANCERS?
NO NO... THE HOTEL ROOM. I COULD HAVE TOLD YOU YOU WOULDN'T NEED ONE OF THOSE...
YES... BY THE TIME WE WERE CHUCKED OUT OF THE LAST STRIP JOINT IT WAS TIME TO GO TO THE AIRPORT FOR THE 6AM FLIGHT HOME...

Alex
BEATTIE + TAYLOR
GOOD NEWS, HOLLIS?
YES. LOOK EVERYONE... THE RESULTS OF MY SFA EXAMS HAVE COME THROUGH AND I'VE PASSED!
I'M NO LONGER A TRAINEE FIT ONLY FOR PHOTOCOPYING AND COFFEE-MAKING. AS OF TODAY I'M LICENSED TO TRANSACT BUSINESS AND DEAL WITH CLIENTS DIRECTLY...
SPLENDID NEWS. I THINK THIS CALLS FOR A BOTTLE OR TWO OF BUBBLY DOWN AT THE WINE BAR. WHAT DO YOU SAY, LADS?
I'LL GET MY JACKET...
ER... NOT YOU, HOLLIS. WE'RE OFFICIALLY ALLOWED TO LEAVE YOU MANNING THE PHONES DURING LUNCH NOW...
NONE OF US NEED TO WORRY ABOUT WHEN IT'S GOING TO BE OUR TURN AGAIN... HOORAY!
YEE HAH!

POP

Alex
BEATTIE + TAYLOR
WELL, CLIVE, I CAN SEE YOU'VE BEEN TRYING TO INGRATIATE YOURSELF WITH ME AS YOUR NEW BOSS.. AND THIS MEETING IS JUST ANOTHER PRETEXT...
TRYING TO CHARM THE NEW WOMAN WITH YOUR CHIVALROUS GENTLEMANLY ATTENTIONS... BUT THIS RAISES CERTAIN MATTERS OF ETIQUETTE WHICH MIGHT BE DEEMED PATRONISING... I'M REFERRING TO THE OPENING OF DOORS...
OH... THAT, ER...
THINK ABOUT IT, CLIVE... IF ONE IS GOING FOR A MEETING AND SOMEONE POINTEDLY ENSURES THE DOOR IS OPENED THAT'S BEHAVIOUR DESIGNED TO MAKE ONE FEEL INFERIOR HUMILIATED AND INSIGNIFICANT, ISN'T IT?
WELL... IF YOU PUT IT THAT WAY...
I'VE LEFT MY DOOR AJAR, CLIVE... PAY ATTENTION...
OH GOD...
A SIGNAL TO THE WHOLE OFFICE THAT YOU'RE NOT TAKING ME REMOTELY SERIOUSLY...

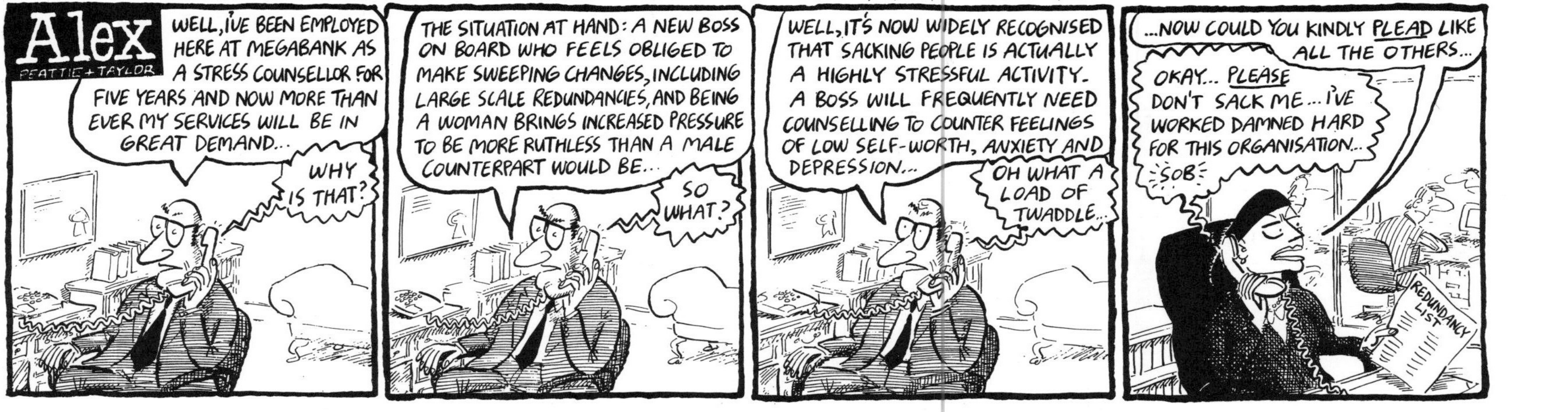
Alex
BEATTIE + TAYLOR
WELL, I'VE BEEN EMPLOYED HERE AT MEGABANK AS A STRESS COUNSELLOR FOR FIVE YEARS AND NOW MORE THAN EVER MY SERVICES WILL BE IN GREAT DEMAND...
WHY IS THAT?
THE SITUATION AT HAND: A NEW BOSS ON BOARD WHO FEELS OBLIGED TO MAKE SWEEPING CHANGES, INCLUDING LARGE SCALE REDUNDANCIES, AND BEING A WOMAN BRINGS INCREASED PRESSURE TO BE MORE RUTHLESS THAN A MALE COUNTERPART WOULD BE...
SO WHAT?
WELL, IT'S NOW WIDELY RECOGNISED THAT SACKING PEOPLE IS ACTUALLY A HIGHLY STRESSFUL ACTIVITY. A BOSS WILL FREQUENTLY NEED COUNSELLING TO COUNTER FEELINGS OF LOW SELF-WORTH, ANXIETY AND DEPRESSION...
OH WHAT A LOAD OF TWADDLE...
...NOW COULD YOU KINDLY PLEAD LIKE ALL THE OTHERS...
OKAY... PLEASE DON'T SACK ME... I'VE WORKED DAMNED HARD FOR THIS ORGANISATION...
SOB
REDUNDANCY LIST

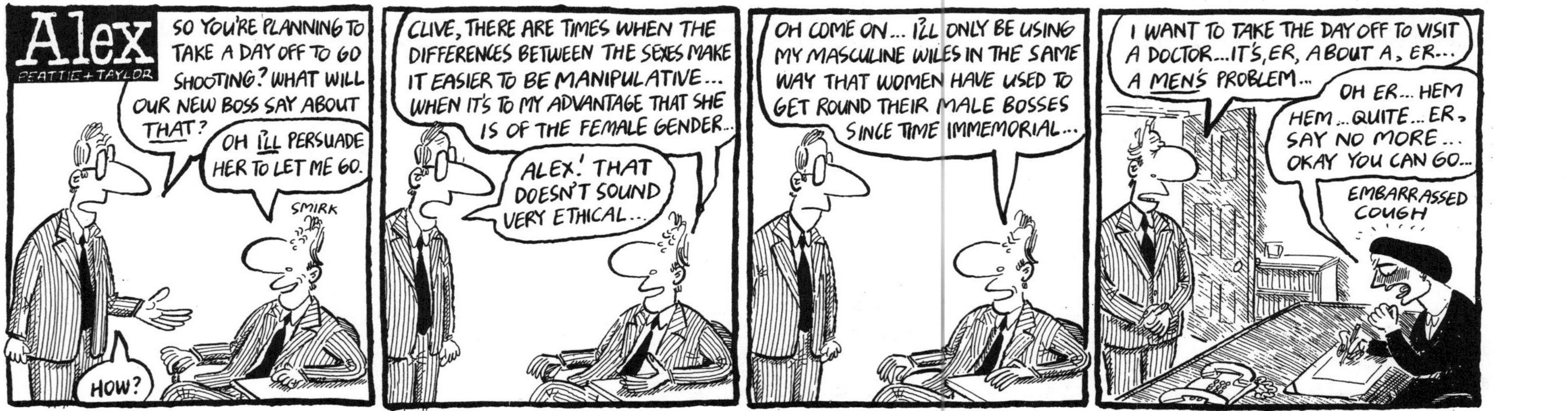
Alex
BEATTIE + TAYLOR
SO YOU'RE PLANNING TO TAKE A DAY OFF TO GO SHOOTING? WHAT WILL OUR NEW BOSS SAY ABOUT THAT?
OH I'LL PERSUADE HER TO LET ME GO.
SMIRK
HOW?
CLIVE, THERE ARE TIMES WHEN THE DIFFERENCES BETWEEN THE SEXES MAKE IT EASIER TO BE MANIPULATIVE... WHEN IT'S TO MY ADVANTAGE THAT SHE IS OF THE FEMALE GENDER...
ALEX! THAT DOESN'T SOUND VERY ETHICAL...
OH COME ON... I'LL ONLY BE USING MY MASCULINE WILES IN THE SAME WAY THAT WOMEN HAVE USED TO GET ROUND THEIR MALE BOSSES SINCE TIME IMMEMORIAL...
I WANT TO TAKE THE DAY OFF TO VISIT A DOCTOR... IT'S, ER, ABOUT A, ER... A MEN'S PROBLEM...
OH ER... HEM HEM... QUITE... ER, SAY NO MORE... OKAY YOU CAN GO...
EMBARRASSED COUGH

Alex
BEATTIE + TAYLOR
YOU'RE WORKING HARD... BUT THE REST OF THE CITY IS WINDING DOWN FOR CHRISTMAS...
TSK. YOU GRADUATE TRAINEES KNOW NOTHING ABOUT THE FINANCIAL WORLD...
YOU THINK WE ANALYSTS SHOULD SIMPLY STOP PUBLISHING MARKET REPORTS?.. WHEN PEOPLE ARE HAVING TO MAKE CRUCIAL MAJOR FINANCIAL DECISIONS, WHO NEED TO BE PROVIDED WITH AN ABUNDANCE OF WELL-TIMED RECENT DATA...
WE'RE TALKING ABOUT INDIVIDUALS WHO ARE ENTRUSTED WITH VERY LARGE AMOUNTS OF CAPITAL... OBVIOUSLY THEY HAVE TO HAVE GUIDANCE IN KNOWING WHAT TO DO WITH THE FUNDS THEY'RE IN CHARGE OF...
WHO? THE INVESTMENT MANAGERS WHO HANDLE PENSION MONIES?
NO. OUR BOSSES WHO ALLOCATE OUR XMAS BONUSES...
THIS IS THE TIME WHEN I LIKE TO CHURN OUT AS MUCH BULKY RESEARCH GUFF AS POSSIBLE TO MAKE A GOOD IMPRESSION ON HIM...
TAP
TAP

Alex
PEATTIE + TAYLOR
DID YOU HEAR? - A RUMOUR WENT ROUND THE MARKET YESTERDAY THAT BILL CLINTON HAD COLLAPSED AND DIED OF A HEART ATTACK WHILE OUT JOGGING...
OF COURSE IT TURNED OUT TO BE TOTALLY UNFOUNDED - NO DOUBT A PIECE OF MISCHIEF DREAMT UP BY SOME TRADER TO GET HIMSELF OUT OF AN AWKWARD CURRENCY POSITION.
NEVERTHELESS IT MUST HAVE CAUSED SERIOUS INCONVENIENCE.
OH YES. BELIEVING IT TO BE TRUE, OUR TRADERS WERE DIVERTED FOR A WHOLE HALF HOUR INTO ULTIMATELY USELESS AND COUNTER-PRODUCTIVE ACTIVITY.
TRYING TO BE THE FIRST TO THINK UP A BAD TASTE JOKE ON THE SUBJECT TO REGALE THE MARKET WITH?
QUITE. THEY CAME UP WITH A COUPLE OF GOOD 'UNS TOO... PITY REALLY...

Alex
BEATTIE + TAYLOR
HONESTLY! THAT ALEX! WHY DO MEN LIKE HIM HAVE TO BE SO OBVIOUS? HE'S SO UNSUBTLE IT'S EMBARRASSING....
OH DEAR... WHAT'S GOING ON...?
WELL, HE KEEPS TRYING TO FIND EXCUSES TO BE ALONE WITH ME AT THE WORKPLACE... CATCH ME IN DARK CORNERS, TRAP ME IN THE FILING ROOM, SIT NEXT TO ME AT ANY OPPORTUNITY AND HASSLE ME TO GO FOR A QUIET DRINK TOGETHER...
OH DEAR...
WELL I'M AFRAID THAT'S HOW SOME MEN REACT WHEN THEY FIND THEMSELVES WORKING FOR A SEXUALLY AVAILABLE WOMAN... THEY'VE JUST GOT ONE THING ON THEIR MIND YOU SEE... THEY'RE COMPLETELY INSENSITIVE TO HOW IT MIGHT MAKE HER FEEL...
WHAT, A BIT FRISKY, LIKE ME?
YES... BUT ALL THEY'RE THINKING ABOUT IS LOBBYING FOR THEIR BLOOMING BONUSES AT THIS TIME OF YEAR... TYPICAL!
I KNOW! MEN!!

Alex
BEATTIE + TAYLOR
I THOUGHT THAT GETTING EACH OF MY STAFF TO PROVIDE ME WITH A CURRENT C.V. WOULD BE A GOOD WAY OF FINDING OUT MORE ABOUT THEM...
ACTUALLY IT DOESN'T REALLY HELP MUCH... ALEX FOR EXAMPLE WAS VERY PROMPT IN SUPPLYING ME WITH THE MOST IMPRESSIVE AND FULLY UP-TO-DATE RESUMÉ
BUT IT'S FRUSTRATING WHAT IT DOESN'T TELL ME... I FEEL I'D LIKE TO KNOW MORE ABOUT THE INDIVIDUAL'S PERSONAL PSYCHOLOGY BEFORE I'D BE ABLE TO FORM A PROPER JUDGEMENT FROM THIS...
YES... I KNOW WHAT YOU MEAN...
MIGHT HE BE TOO STUPID TO REALISE THAT HAVING A CURRENT C.V. ON FILE SHOWS HE'S DISLOYALLY LOOKING FOR ANOTHER POSITION..?
...OR IS HE DELIBERATELY SUGGESTING HE'S ACTIVELY JOB-SEEKING TO PRESSURISE ME INTO GIVING HIM A BIGGER BONUS...?
HMMM...

Alex
PEATTIE + TAYLOR
EVERYONE TOLD US THAT HAVING A FEMALE HEAD OF DEPARTMENT WOULD BE A ROUND-THE-CLOCK NIGHTMARE...
AND THAT WOMEN IN POSITIONS OF POWER IMPOSE A MUCH MORE AUTHORITARIAN AND DISCIPLINARIAN REGIME THAN MEN...BUT IN CERTAIN AREAS I FEEL THINGS ARE MORE RELAXED THAN WHEN RUPERT WAS IN CHARGE...
IN FACT EVER SINCE JANE TOOK OVER I FIND MYSELF COMING IN TO THE OFFICE WITH A SPRING IN MY STEP IN A MOOD OF JOYFUL ANTICIPATION...
OF A PLEASANT 45 MINUTES SPENT READING THE PAPERS IN THE LOO?
EXACTLY...ZERO CHANCE OF THE BOSS WALKING IN AND CATCHING US...

BRRR BRRR...
RING RING
MEN

Alex
PEATTIE + TAYLOR
OF COURSE IN THE DAYS BEFORE E-MAIL A COMPLEX INFRASTRUCTURE OF MESSENGERS AND SECRETARIES WAS REQUIRED TO PHYSICALLY DELIVER FILES, DOCUMENTS, MEMOS ETC BETWEEN DEPARTMENTS...
WHEREAS THESE DAYS ALL EMPLOYEES HAVE COMPUTERS WHICH ARE LINKED TOGETHER IN A HIGHLY SOPHISTICATED NETWORK, ENABLING THE INSTANTANEOUS ELECTRONIC TRANSFER OF DATA TO ANYWHERE IN THE BUILDING...
A TECHNOLOGICAL INNOVATION DESIGNED TO CUT DOWN ON THE NECESSITY FOR BANK PERSONNEL TO WASTE THEIR TIME SCURRYING AROUND FROM DEPARTMENT TO DEPARTMENT...
EXCEPT IN CLIVE'S CASE...
AH YES...
...SECRETLY PRINTING OUT HIS C.V. FOR A JOB APPLICATION AND IT HASN'T APPEARED ON ANY OF THE PRINTERS ON OUR FLOOR?
HE'D BETTER FIND WHICH ONE IT'S BEEN ROUTED THROUGH TO.... BEFORE SOMEONE ELSE DOES...

Alex
PEATTIE + TAYLOR
SO DID YOU HAVE A GOOD HOLIDAY, PAULA?
YES, THANKS. AND I SUPPOSE CHRIS, MY BOSS, HAS JUST GONE OFF ON HIS HOLS...
YES. HE ASKED ME TO SEE YOU ON YOUR RETURN. WELL, YOU KNOW HOW HELPLESS AND WISHY-WASHY HE IS AND HOW YOU, AS HIS SECRETARY, RUN HIS LIFE FOR HIM..
YES. IT'S THE FIRST TIME I HAVEN'T BEEN AT HIS SIDE IN THE OFFICE.
I KNOW. AND ACTUALLY I THINK IT WAS RATHER THOUGHTLESS OF YOU TO TAKE YOUR HOLIDAY AT A SEPARATE TIME FROM HIM. YOU MUST HAVE KNOWN THERE WERE CERTAIN THINGS HE WAS INCAPABLE OF DOING FOR HIMSELF...
...SUCH AS SACKING YOU... AND NOW HE'S BEEN ABLE TO DELEGATE IT TO ME IN HIS ABSENCE.
P45
THE WIMP. I NEVER THOUGHT HE HAD IT IN HIM...

Alex
PEATTIE + TAYLOR
SO YOU'RE HAVING LUNCH WITH ALEX?
YES. TOMORROW.
HOW DID HE MANAGE TO ACHIEVE THAT?
OH, PERSUASION, FLIRTATION AND CHARM I GUESS, PLUS PERSISTENCE AND WHEEDLING. HE KNEW HOW TO GET TO ME IN THE END... TO BE HONEST I RESPECT A MAN WHO KNOWS HOW TO SWEET-TALK A LADY...
ESPECIALLY IF THE WOMAN IN QUESTION, BY VIRTUE OF HER POSITION IN THE COMPANY, HAS A REPUTATION FOR BEING TOUGH, UNYIELDING UNSENTIMENTAL, ALOOF, DISDAINFUL EVEN...
YES INDEED...
YOUR SECRETARY REALLY HAS TO FIGHT OFF EMPLOYEES TRYING TO SCHEDULE LUNCH WITH THE BOSS IN THE RUN UP TO BONUS TIME.
GETTING THEIR NAME IN THE BOOK REALLY SORTS OUT THE MEN FROM THE BOYS...
DIARY
DIARY
1996

Alex
BEATTIE + TAYLOR
HEY, WATCH WHO YOU GIVE THE BILL TO...ARE YOU MAKING ASSUMPTIONS ABOUT ME BECAUSE I'M A WOMAN? THAT MAKES ME SO CROSS...
OH ER... SORRY.. I DIDN'T THINK ..ER...
MAYBE YOU SHOULD ASK WHICH OF US IS PICKING UP THE TAB... I'LL HAVE YOU KNOW I'M A SENIOR DIRECTOR AT MEGABANK AND THE ONLY PEOPLE I ANSWER TO ARE THE CHIEF EXECUTIVE AND THE CHAIRMAN..
WHEREAS THIS GENTLEMAN IS ACTUALLY A SUBORDINATE EMPLOYEE AT THE BANK ANSWERABLE DIRECTLY TO ME...
ER ...SO..?
SO GIVE HIM THE BILL AND I'LL AUTHORISE ITS PAYMENT WHEN IT'S SUBMITTED TO ME ON HIS EXPENSES CLAIM...
ER... RIGHT YOU ARE, MADAM...
SEETHE

Alex
BEATTIE + TAYLOR
SO YOU FINALLY GOT THE INFORMATION YOU NEEDED FOR THIS GROMEX STORY?
YES... BUT NO THANKS TO THEIR PROFESSIONAL ADVISERS I CAN TELL YOU...
DAILY BUGLE CITY DEPT
I MUST HAVE SPOKEN TO HALF THE PEOPLE IN THEIR P.R. FIRM... ALL USELESS... YOU RANT AND RAVE, TELL THEM YOU'RE UP AGAINST A DEADLINE BUT ALL YOU GET ARE EXCUSES, STALLING, UNCOOPERATIVENESS, INDECISION...
I HAD TO PHONE AT LEAST EIGHT TIMES BEFORE I FINALLY GOT THROUGH TO A PERSON WITH THE RIGHT LEVEL OF AUTHORITY TO RELEASE THIS DOCUMENT TO ME...
THE GRADUATE TRAINEE?
YEAH... THEIR CLIENT'S HIGHLY PRICE-SENSITIVE DRAFT RESULTS FIGURES AND HE FAXED THEM OVER LIKE A LAMB...
GROMEX DRAFT RESULTS

Alex
BEATTIE + TAYLOR
I REMEMBER WHEN I WAS A KID MY DAD RANTING ON ABOUT THE DELETERIOUS EFFECTS OF T.V. ON THE YOUNGER GENERATION. I'M BEGINNING TO UNDERSTAND WHAT HE MEANT.
COFFEE
TEA
CHOCOLATE
I MEAN, ONCE THERE WAS A TIME WHEN PEOPLE WERE FORCED TO FIND ACTIVE WAYS TO ENTERTAIN THEMSELVES, USING THEIR BRAINS AND BODIES, AND IN THE PROCESS DEVELOPING USEFUL SKILLS...
BUT THESE DAYS I DON'T KNOW WHAT'S COME OVER PEOPLE; THEY JUST SLUMP THEMSELVES IN A CHAIR IN FRONT OF THE SCREEN, SWITCH OFF THEIR BRAINS AND EXPECT TO BE PASSIVELY ENTERTAINED.
I KNOW WHAT YOU MEAN...
...GAWPING AT THEIR SCREEN-SAVERS TO WHILE AWAY A DULL AFTERNOON...
I MEAN, IN OUR DAY WE USED TO PLAY COMPUTER GOLF OR FIGHTER COMBAT...
...LOOK WHAT THE LITTLE SQUIRREL IS DOING NOW...

Alex
BEATTIE + TAYLOR
YOU CAN REALLY SEE WHO THE GO-GETTERS ARE OUT THERE CAN'T YOU?
YES... LOOK AT THE WAY KEVIN REALLY THROWS HIMSELF INTO HIS TRADING...
AT TIMES LIKE THIS WHEN BUSINESS IS A BIT QUIET A LOT OF PEOPLE JUST WIND DOWN AND GET UNMOTIVATED...
BUT NOT KEVIN.
NO...
AND IF THERE'S ONE NON-APATHETIC INDIVIDUAL LIKE HIM WHO IS GETTING OUT THERE MAKING LOTS OF CALLS; SHOWING ENTHUSIASM AND ENERGY.. OBVIOUSLY THAT CAN BE REALLY GOOD FOR THE MORALLE OF THOSE ROUND HIM AND LIFTS THEIR SPIRITS...
INDEED...
...SEEING SOMEONE WHO IS STILL TRYING TO GET HIS BOOK IN PROFIT IN TIME FOR A BONUS...HEE HEE!
IT CHEERS EVERYONE UP...
PSST... WE'VE ALL MADE OUR MONEY AND WE'RE SITTING ON OUR HANDS.
WHAT A LOSER! HA HA

Alex
PEATTIE + TAYLOR
OF COURSE THINGS CAN BE TOUGH FOR OUR NEW BOSS JANE... IT'S NOT JUST THAT AS A WOMAN SHE IS DEBARRED FROM ENTERING TRADITIONAL CITY CLUBS LIKE THIS...
IN MANY OTHER RESPECTS WOMEN COME UP AGAINST PREJUDICES AND PRESUMPTIONS ABOUT THEIR STATUS FROM MEN. EVEN WHEN THEY'RE ACTUALLY POWERFUL EXECUTIVES.
FOR EXAMPLE THERE ARE STILL PEOPLE IN THE CITY WHO WILL MAKE AN INSTINCTIVE, ALBEIT ERRONEOUS JUDGEMENT WHEN THEY PICK UP THE PHONE AND HEAR A WOMAN'S VOICE AT THE OTHER END...
YES INDEED.
AND NOT PUT HER THROUGH UNDER ANY CIRCUMSTANCES IN CASE IT'S ONE'S WIFE...
NO, MADAM, I HAVEN'T SEEN MR MASTERLEY TODAY.
EXCELLENT. WE'RE SAFE FOR ANOTHER HALF HOUR... BRANDY?

Alex
PEATTIE + TAYLOR
SO WE'RE GOING OUT TO LUNCH WITH OLD JIM? IS THAT WISE?
DON'T WORRY, CLIVE. IT'LL BE A MORE RELAXED OCCASION THAN IT USED TO BE NOW WE'VE FINALLY FOUND A PROPER NICHE FOR HIM...
IT'S OFTEN HARD TO KNOW WHAT TO DO WITH THESE OLD BOYS ONCE THEY'RE GETTING A BIT LONG IN THE TOOTH BUT ARE STILL A FEW YEARS OFF FROM RETIREMENT AGE...
SO, LIKE MANY BANKS DO, WE'VE MADE HIM COMPLIANCE OFFICER. PUTTING HIM IN CHARGE OF OVERSEEING THE HONEST TRANSACTING OF BUSINESS SEEMED FITTING IN VIEW OF HIS 40 YEARS IN THE MARKET...
AH YES... OF COURSE...
IT MEANS HE'LL NO LONGER BE ABLE TO ANNOY US BY ENDLESSLY RECOUNTING STORIES OF ALL THE LUCRATIVE INSIDER DEALS THEY USED TO DO IN THE GOOD OLD DAYS BEFORE THE FINANCIAL SERVICES ACT...
QUITE... LET'S GO...

Alex
PEATTIE + TAYLOR
YOU'RE GOING OUT TO DINNER WITH ALEX?... THIS IS GETTING TO BE MORE THAN A BUSINESS RELATIONSHIP, ISN'T IT?
WELL YES...
OKAY. LISTEN, JANE. THIS IS IMPORTANT...
DO I HAVE TO REMIND YOU THAT YOU'RE HIS BOSS AND YOU ARE EXPECTED TO BE RESPONSIBLE WITH REGARD TO SOCIAL RELATIONSHIPS WITH EMPLOYEES...
WHAT ARE YOU TALKING ABOUT?
FOR GOD'S SAKE, JANE, HE'S MARRIED. ...HE'S GOT A LOVELY WIFE CALLED PENNY WHO YOU'VE MET... AND ALSO THERE'S LITTLE CHRISTOPHER TO CONSIDER... THEIR SON WHO ALEX ADORES.
OH... I SEE... ER, YOU'D BETTER TELL ME ALL...
SO, ER... HOW'S HENNY AND LITTLE CHRISTOPHER? STARTED SCHOOL?
FINE... YES, HE HAS...
AND HOW'S YOUR GOLF? WHAT'S YOUR HANDICAP THESE DAYS?
LOOK, COULD WE CUT THE SMALL TALK, JANE?

Alex
PEATTIE + TAYLOR
SO IT'S MORE THAN JUST SMARMING UP TO THE BOSS?... ALEX HAS DECLARED TO HAVING A SECRET CRUSH ON YOU?
YES. AND HE'S WHO ALL THE FLOWERS ARE FROM...
DON'T TELL ME THAT DOESN'T AROUSE YOUR INTEREST A BIT...?
WELL YES... CALL ME OLD-FASHIONED BUT I THINK THIS SORT OF THING SAYS SOMETHING ABOUT A MAN... IT MEANS A LOT TO ME...
I MEAN, WHEN A CHAP KEEPS SENDING FLOWERS AND CHOCOLATES AND ALWAYS GETS TABLES IN THE BEST RESTAURANTS FOR MEALS TOGETHER, TICKETS FOR THE THEATRE ETC... WELL, I HAVE TO SAY HE'S A GUY WHO'S GOT WHAT IT IS I NEED.
GO ON... CALL HIS NUMBER NOW!
OKAY.
EGAD! SHE'S POACHED MY SECRETARY!
BOY, THAT WOMAN IS SO SHARP ISN'T SHE? SHE DOESN'T MISS A TRICK...
NO WONDER I WORSHIP HER.

Alex
BEATTIE + TAYLOR
SEEING THIS NEW BATCH OF GRADUATE TRAINEES MAKES ME AWARE OF HOW MUCH I'VE LEARNED IN MY YEAR IN THE CITY...
WHEN ONE FIRST ARRIVES ONE IS SO IGNORANT, YET SO PRESUMPTUOUS... I REALISE I WASN'T REALLY ABLE TO APPRECIATE SOME OF THE FUNDAMENTAL TRUTHS YOU WERE TRYING TO IMBUE IN ME, ALEX...
AFTER ALL, WHEN I CAME IN EACH MORNING AND ASKED HOW THE MARKETS WERE YOU'D ALWAYS TAKE THE TROUBLE TO REPLY... AND NOW I FEEL I AM ABLE TO PASS ON YOUR WISE AND JUST WORDS TO A NEW GENERATION.
SO HOW ARE THE MARKETS?
OH, JUST SHUT UP AND GO AND GET US OUR COFFEE...
IT MAKES YOU CRINGE TO REALISE YOU WERE ONCE THAT IRRITATING DOESN'T IT?

Alex
BEATTIE + TAYLOR
LOOK, JANE, ...THERE'S SOMETHING I WANT TO ASK YOU... SOMETHING I MUST KNOW...
OH NO... DON'T SAY IT, ALEX...DON'T SPOIL IT... WE'VE BEEN HAVING SUCH A NICE EVENING...
NO... I'VE TRIED TO RESTRAIN MYSELF BUT IT'S NOT FAIR, YOU SITTING ACROSS THE TABLE FROM ME, MAKING SMALL TALK... ME HAVING TO PRETEND WE'RE JUST GOOD FRIENDS, HAVING TO ACCEPT THIS BARRIER BETWEEN US...
I CAN'T GO ON LIKE THIS...AM I WASTING MY TIME WITH YOU?...ARE YOU GOING TO GIVE ME A SIGN? CAN'T YOU GIVE ME ANY ENCOURAGEMENT...? YOU KNOW WHAT YOU ARE TO ME...
YES. YES, I DO. OF COURSE...
YOUR BOSS... AND DON'T YOU FORGET IT...
EXACTLY. COME ON, WHAT'S MY BONUS? GIMME A HINT... PLEASE...
HEH, HEH, HEH... WAIT AND SEE...

FOOTSIE
FOOTSIE

Alex
PEATTIE + TAYLOR
ALEX, IT'S JANE...LOOK I JUST WANT TO TELL YOU I'VE BOOKED A ROOM... SOMEWHERE NICE AND DISCREET...
OKAY... YES...
A PRIVATE LITTLE ROOM THAT NO-ONE ELSE KNOWS ABOUT...A PLACE WHERE ONE KNOWS THAT ONE ISN'T GOING TO BE DISTURBED...WHERE ONE CAN FEEL SAFE FROM PRYING EYES AND TATTLING TONGUES...
ALRIGHT... WHERE? WHEN?
I BET YOU CAN GUESS WHAT I'M LOOKING FORWARD TO DOING IN THAT ROOM, ALEX...AND I'M SURE YOU'D LIKE TO JOIN ME... WOULDN'T YOU, ALEX?...
YES...
YES...
BUT YOU CAN'T, BECAUSE THE ANNUAL SALARY REVIEW AND BONUS ASSESSMENT HAS TO BE CONDUCTED IN TOTAL SECRECY... CLICK
BIFF
SOB
OH MY GOD... SHE IS SUCH A TEASE...

Alex
PEATTIE + TAYLOR
SO DRUMMOND SUFFERS FROM "ROAD RAGE"... I'VE WORKED WITH HIM FOR YEARS AND HE ALWAYS SEEMED THE MOST LEVEL-HEADED, SENSIBLE, PLACID SORT OF CHAP...
YET AS SOON AS HE GRIPS A STEERING WHEEL HIS KNUCKLES WHITEN AND HE BECOMES AN AGGRESSIVE, CONFRONTATIONAL COMPETITIVE ROAD HOG, ENGAGING IN PETTY SPEED CONTESTS WITH ANY DRIVER WHO TRIES TO OVERTAKE HIM...
YOU AND I OF COURSE WILL NATURALLY EXERCISE SELF-CONTROL, PROCEEDING ALONG AT A SENSIBLE SEDATE PACE, SHOWING CONSIDERATION TO OTHER DRIVERS AND GRACIOUSLY PULLING OVER TO ALLOW THEM TO PASS SHOULD THEY WISH...
DRUMMOND REALLY HAS GOT TO SORT HIMSELF OUT...
...IF HE EVER WINS OUR CORPORATE GO-KARTING DAY AHEAD OF ALL OUR CLIENTS AGAIN HE'S SACKED...

Alex
PEATTIE + TAYLOR
GOD THAT WAS AN AWFUL THING TO HAPPEN... I FEEL SO ASHAMED AND HUMILIATED...THAT'S RUINED EVERYTHING... MY LIFE IS DESTROYED...
DON'T MAKE SUCH A BIG DEAL OUT OF IT...
THAT'S THE ULTIMATE NIGHTMARE... GOING OUT ON A ROMANTIC ENCOUNTER WITH ONE'S NEW LADY-FRIEND AT A DELICATE STAGE IN THE RELATIONSHIP AND THEN THAT HAPPENS...
ALEX, YOU WORRY TOO MUCH...
WE MEET SOMEONE WHO'S KNOWN ME PERSONALLY FOR YEARS...SOMEONE WHO KNOWS MY WIFE... WHO KNOWS ABOUT MY SON CHRISTOPHER AND KNOWS THE PEOPLE I WORK WITH...AND IS BASICALLY ONE OF MY OLDEST ACQUAINTANCES...
AND THEN HE PRETENDS HE DOESN'T RECOGNISE ME - B*ST**D!
HE WAS PROBABLY TRYING TO BE DISCREET, ALEX...
BUT I ONLY BROUGHT YOU HERE BECAUSE I HAVE SUCH A GOOD RELATIONSHIP WITH THE MAÎTRE D'...

Alex
PEATTIE + TAYLOR
HOTEL
LOOK, ALEX, IF WE'RE GOING TO SPEND THE NIGHT TOGETHER I'M RELYING ON YOU TO BE RESPONSIBLE ABOUT... YOU HAVE GOT THE NECESSARY... ER?
OH... DON'T YOU HAVE ANY ER...?
NO OF COURSE NOT... DO I LOOK LIKE ONE OF THE SORT OF WOMEN WHO CARRY THEM?
ER... NO...
ALL I WANT TO KNOW IS WHAT KIND OF PRECAUTIONS YOU INTEND TAKING WITH REGARDS TO SEX...
I KNOW HOW TEMPTING IT IS TO IGNORE CERTAIN THINGS BECAUSE OF HOW IT IS AT THE CRUCIAL TIME IN THE HEAT OF THE MOMENT... WHEN YOU'RE TURNED ON AND...
DON'T WORRY. I'M EQUIPPED...
AND I WON'T TURN IT OFF AND IF IT RINGS I WILL ANSWER IT. OKAY?
GOOD... I MEAN IT MIGHT BE SOMEONE REALLY IMPORTANT FROM WORK...

Alex
PEATTIE + TAYLOR
LOOK, THIS IS THE FIRST TIME WE'RE GOING TO SLEEP TOGETHER... I'VE GOT TO TELL YOU I FEEL A BIT ANXIOUS...
YOU DO? WHY?
THERE'S ALL THIS PRESSURE, JANE, TO SHOW YOU WHAT KIND OF MAN I AM... WHATEVER HAPPENS YOU WILL STILL RESPECT ME IN THE MORNING WON'T YOU...?
OF COURSE... DON'T WORRY... COME TO BED...
I MEAN, LIKE, WHAT I DO WITH YOU WHEN I GET INTO BED WITH YOU... YOU KNOW, I FEEL LIKE MY PERFORMANCE IS BEING JUDGED NOW.
DON'T BE SILLY... SHUSH...
SO YOU WON'T THINK ANY THE WORSE OF ME IF I DON'T FALL ASLEEP IMMEDIATELY THROUGH OVERWORK?
NO NO... JUST FORGET ABOUT YOUR BONUS FOR A FEW MINUTES...

Alex
PEATTIE + TAYLOR
I'VE GOT TO TELL YOU I'M STARTING TO GET EXTREMELY WORRIED ABOUT ALEX'S BEHAVIOUR...
I'M AFRAID HE MIGHT BE ABOUT TO SERIOUSLY MAKE A FOOL OF HIMSELF OVER HIS RELATIONSHIP WITH OUR NEW FEMALE BOSS JANE...
...LOOK HOW HE'S BEEN WRITING HER NAME OBSESSIVELY OVER AND OVER AGAIN ON HIS BLOTTER...
YOU THINK HE MIGHT HAVE BECOME INFATUATED WITH HER?
NO, I'M WORRIED THAT HE MIGHT HAVE AGREED TO SIGN ALL HER XMAS CARDS FOR HER OUT OF SHEER BONUS-TIME CRAWLING...

Alex
PEATTIE + TAYLOR
THE FACT THAT ALMOST EVERYONE THESE DAYS HAS A MOBILE PHONE REALLY IS A HUGE BOON TO ONE'S SOCIAL LIFE...
AND WITH THE VAST MEMORY CAPACITY OF THE MODERN MICRO-CHIP ONE CAN HAVE THE NUMBERS OF LITERALLY HUNDREDS OF SOCIAL AND BUSINESS ACQUAINTANCES PRE-PROGRAMMED IN...
LET'S SEE... DEREK HOLMES... "MEMORY RECALL"... AND "DIAL"... HERE WE GO...
PLICK PLICK
email: alex-cartoon@etgate.co.uk
BOOKS
Health
RING RING
AH GOOD... IT IS HIM... I THOUGHT SO... NOW I CAN GO UP AND SAY HELLO...
YOUR CRAVEN TIMIDITY STILL SHOCKS ME AFTER ALL THESE YEARS, CLIVE...
HELLO?
CLICK

Alex
PEATTIE + TAYLOR
HELL! AS SOON AS SMEDLEY HAD BANKED HIS BONUS CHEQUE HE'S RESIGNED TO GO TO ANOTHER JOB...
OH DEAR. THAT'S A BLOW: LOSING ONE OF YOUR BEST PEOPLE LIKE THAT...
WHAT ARE YOU GOING TO DO? MAKE HIM WORK OUT HIS THREE MONTHS' NOTICE HERE AT LEAST..?
OH NO... WHAT'S THE POINT? IT'S XMAS SEASON, THE OFFICE IS WINDING DOWN... NO-ONE REALLY WORKS MUCH UNTIL THE NEW YEAR ANYWAY... IT WON'T DO ME ANY GOOD KEEPING HIM ON HERE...
I DON'T WANT TO BE SENSELESSLY VINDICTIVE... IT IS CHRISTMAS AFTER ALL... I'LL PHONE HIS NEW BOSS AND SAY SMEDLEY CAN START THERE IMMEDIATELY...
QUITE RIGHT.
AS A NEW BUG SMEDLEY WILL GET LANDED WITH ALL THE LUNCHTIME PHONE ANSWERING DUTIES... HA HA HA...
PLUS THEY'LL PROBABLY LUMBER HIM WITH THE POST-XMAS PRE-NEW YEAR SHIFT EVERYONE ELSE BOOKS HOLIDAYS TO AVOID COMING IN FOR...
HEH HEH HEH...
PLICK... PLICK...

Alex
PEATTIE + TAYLOR
SO, LIKE ALL GRADUATES THESE DAYS YOU'RE A BIT OF A WIZ ON THE OLD P.C. EH, PORTER?
IT'S JUST AN E-MAIL XMAS CARD I'VE KNOCKED UP FOR YOU, ALEX. THEY'RE VERY FASHIONABLE THIS YEAR...
A LITTLE IMAGE OF SANTA APPEARS ON THE RECIPIENT'S SCREEN WITH THE MESSAGE: "SEASON'S GREETINGS FROM ALEX MASTERLEY." AND THE BEAUTY IS YOU CAN SEND IT TO ALL YOUR CLIENTS AT THE TOUCH OF A SINGLE BUTTON.
HMM... MOST INGENIOUS...
I MEAN, JUST THINK OF THE SAVINGS...
I APPRECIATE THAT, PORTER, BUT THERE'S SOMETHING SATISFYING ABOUT THE GOOD OLD-FASHIONED PHYSICAL XMAS CARD THAT'S SENT THROUGH THE POST.
NAMELY MAKING YOU FAKE MY SIGNATURE ON ALL 500... NOW GET DOWN TO IT...
NICE TRY THOUGH...

Alex
BEATTIE + TAYLOR
SO HOW'S ALEX? HE STILL PAYING YOU AS MUCH CONSIDERATION AS EVER...?
ACTUALLY HE'S BEING A BIT EVASIVE AT THE MOMENT.
OH?
HE KEEPS SAYING HE CAN'T MEET ME TONIGHT, MAYBE NEXT WEEK... THAT HE'S GOT A LOT ON; THAT HE DOESN'T KNOW WHEN HE CAN SEE ME...
email: alex-cartoon@etgate.co.uk
IT'S THAT INEVITABLE COOLING OF PASSION WHICH I GUESS ONE SHOULD EXPECT... BASICALLY HE'S TRYING TO TELL ME SOMETHING...
THAT HE'S WORKING REALLY HARD AND DESERVES A BIG BONUS... HE NEVER FORGETS I'M HIS BOSS...
YOU MUST BE SO PROUD OF HIM...

Alex
BEATTIE + TAYLOR
SO TOMORROW WE'RE HOSTING A SPECIAL ONE-DAY CONFERENCE FOR SOME FRENCH CLIENTS?
THAT'S RIGHT. THEY'RE BEING FLOWN OVER FIRST THING...
OF COURSE PAN-EUROPEAN DIGITAL MOBILE PHONE TECHNOLOGY REALLY HAS CHANGED THE FACE OF BUSINESS TRAVEL, ENABLING OFFICES TO KEEP IN CONSTANT CONTACT WITH THEIR EMPLOYEES.
INDEED. UNLIKE THE OLD DAYS.
email: alex-cartoon@etgate.co.uk
REMEMBER, ONE HAD ALL THE INEFFICIENCIES AND VAGARIES OF SWITCHBOARDS, WITH AN OPERATOR FREQUENTLY NOT KNOWING WHERE THE CLIENTS ARE, WHICH EXTENSION TO REACH THEM ON, EVEN WHETHER THEY'VE YET ARRIVED...
EXACTLY.
...WHICH IS JOLLY HANDY WHEN IN FACT THEY'RE SPENDING THE DAY DOING THEIR CHRISTMAS SHOPPING AT HARRODS.
COULD THIS SPELL THE END OF THE BOGUS DECEMBER CONFERENCE AS WE KNOW IT?

Alex
PEATTIE + TAYLOR
WHOOPS. LOOK AT KATE. IN LATE AND HUNG OVER AGAIN...
WELL... THAT'S TO BE EXPECTED AT CHRISTMAS. EVERYONE WANTS TO GO OUT CELEBRATING...
AND AT THIS TIME OF YEAR IT'S NORMAL FOR SOMEONE LIKE HER TO GET INVITED OUT A LOT BY PEOPLE SHE KNOWS THROUGH WORK...
YES BUT SHE'LL BE IN BIG TROUBLE IF SHE GOES ON LIKE THIS...
email: alex-cartoon@etgate.co.uk
I MEAN, HAS SHE FORGOTTEN THAT OUR OFFICE EMPLOYS AN ATTENDANCE SECRETARY TO KEEP METICULOUS DAY-TO-DAY RECORDS OF ALL EMPLOYEES' LATENESSES AND ABSENCES
YOU'RE RIGHT... HER LITTLE SLIPS ARE BOUND TO SHOW UP IN THE REGISTER...
SHE HASN'T MARKED ANYONE ABSENT IN IT FOR TWO WEEKS...
ATTENDANCE REGISTER
WHOSE TURN IS IT TO TAKE HER OUT AND GET HER SMASHED TONIGHT?
ER... GROAN SORRY BUT WERE YOU IN YESTERDAY MORNING?
'COURSE.
SO WAS I!
ME TOO

Alex
BEATTIE + TAYLOR
NO! DON'T TELL ME YOU AND ALEX ARE GOING TO SPLIT UP?
WELL THINGS AREN'T GOING WELL... WE'VE LOST OUR "ZING"... I HAVEN'T SAID ANYTHING TO HIM YET BUT...
SURELY IT DOESN'T HAVE TO END LIKE THAT...?
TINA, THE ROMANCE HAS GONE... I MEAN THE TROUBLE IS WE'RE BOTH STRESSED-OUT PROFESSIONAL PEOPLE AND...
LOOK, MAYBE WHAT YOU NEED IS TO GET AWAY FROM IT ALL SOMEWHERE YOU CAN FORGET ABOUT BOTH YOUR SITUATIONS... A LOT OF PEOPLE FIND A HOLIDAY WORKS WONDERS FOR THEM... THINK ABOUT IT...
email: alex-cartoon@etgate.co.uk
I MEAN, THE BANK HAS PLACES AVAILABLE TO GO ON A CONFERENCE TRIP TO BARBADOS NEXT MONTH... SURELY THAT COULD BE THE PERFECT OPPORTUNITY...
YOU MEAN?..
YES!
...YOU CAN DELEGATE DUMPING HIM TO SOMEONE ELSE WHILE YOU'RE AWAY ON YOUR TOD... THAT'S HOW I ALWAYS SACK PEOPLE...
OH YES. GOOD IDEA.

Alex
PEATTIE + TAYLOR
I'M AFRAID OUR COLLEAGUE PETER HAS GOT A BIT TIPSY AND HAS BEEN TRYING TO PRESS HIS ATTENTIONS ON THAT YOUNG LADY...
GET LOST.
AND SHE JUST DOESN'T WANT TO KNOW?..
YES... IT'S THE USUAL STORY... CORPORATE XMAS PARTY; TOO MUCH DRINK; PEOPLE LETTING THEIR HAIR DOWN AND MISBEHAVING... BUT SHOULD ONE INTERVENE?..
GO AWAY.
HMMM...
LOOK, WHEN SOMEONE CRUDELY AND INAPPROPRIATELY SEXUALLY MOLESTS ANOTHER GUEST: WELL, I THINK THAT PERSON NEEDS TAKING ASIDE AND BEING GIVEN A DAMN GOOD TALKING-TO...
YOU'RE RIGHT.
AND WE LAWYERS ARE EXACTLY THE RIGHT PEOPLE TO GIVE HER THAT...
GOOD OLD PETER... HAS HE GOT HIS BUSINESS CARD OUT YET?
LOOK I SAW HIM GROPE YOUR BUM... LET'S SUE THE B*ST**D...
I TOLD YOU... I DIDN'T MIND... IT WAS UNDER THE MISTLETOE...

Alex
PEATTIE + TAYLOR
I UNDERSTAND THAT ONE OF THE GRADUATE TRAINEES HAD A BIT OF A GO AT YOU AT THE XMAS PARTY...
PHILLIPS? OH JUST THE USUAL DRINK-FUELLED REBELLIOUSNESS. IT'S BEEN SAFELY QUELLED...
email: alex-cartoon@etgate.co.uk
A FAIRLY PREDICTABLE TURN OF EVENTS: HE'D BEEN KNOCKING BACK THE FREE CHAMPAGNE ALL EVENING, HE STAGGERED UP TO ME, SCARCELY COHERENT, AND TOOK ME TO TASK FOR HUMILIATING HIM ABOUT THE OFFICE.
HE SAID I'D BEEN GETTING HIM TO RUN ERRANDS OF A PERSONAL NATURE FOR MYSELF WHICH HE DID NOT CONSIDER TO BE HIS RESPONSIBILITY OR DUTY...
SO WHAT SORT OF ERRANDS DID HE REFUSE TO DO IN FUTURE?
WELL, HE MENTIONED PICKING UP MY DRY CLEANING...
ER... YOUR DRY CLEANING, ALEX.
THANKYOU, PHILLIPS...
...OF COURSE THAT WAS SHORTLY BEFORE HE THREW UP OVER MY JACKET.

Alex
PEATTIE + TAYLOR
EMAIL From: Jane To: All staff Subject: My Departure. CC: — Attachments: —
TAP TAP
TAP
"I regret to announce that after a full and frank discussion with the board I have been left with no option but to resign my position here."
TAP TAP
"I shall be leaving the bank with immediate effect. However I should like to take this opportunity to show my appreciation of how you have received me in my short time here at Megabank."
TAP TAP
email: alex-cartoon@etgate.co.uk
"Each and every one of you has shown me kindness, warmth, respect, personal support, encouragement, loyalty, hospitality and friendship..."
"...all of which is now completely down the drain as someone else will be determining your bonuses... ha ha and so long... Jane."
***!
***!
MASTERFUL IN ALL SHE DOES... SIGH I SHALL MISS HER...

SORRY... WHAT WAS THAT? YOU'RE BREAKING UP...
NO,.... BZZZZ... WRRR.... SSST.... WE'RE BREAKING UP.... BZZZZ...

Alex
PEATTIE + TAYLOR
MORNING, JANE! WHAT'S THAT, YOUR WEEKEND CASE?
ER...YES, I'M GOING ON HOLIDAY ONCE I LEAVE THIS AFTERNOON...
RECEPTION
LUG
HEAVE
email: alex-cartoon@etgate.co.uk
LET ME CARRY THAT. IT LOOKS REALLY HEAVY.
NO. NAFF OFF, CLIVE. I DON'T NEED YOUR PATRONISING HELP. I CAN MANAGE THIS.
ULP. SORRY
THAT WAS TOUGH, JANE...
THIS IS MY LAST DAY IN THIS JOB BUT I STILL HAVE APPEARANCES TO CONSIDER... I'M A PROFESSIONAL FEMALE EXECUTIVE. IF HE CARRIED THIS CASE FOR ME WHAT WOULD IT LOOK LIKE?
LIFT
ER... AS LIGHT AS A FEATHER, I GUESS... AND EMPTY...
QUITE. IN SUSPICIOUS CONTRAST TO WHEN I USE IT TO LUG HOME ALL THE BANK'S CLIENT FILES WHEN I LEAVE HERE LATER...
TOSS
CATCH

Alex
PEATTIE + TAYLOR
LOOK WHAT I GOT FROM A CLIENT: A CRATE OF CLARET. NICE.. BUT IT'S NOT EXACTLY BOLLINGER, IS IT?
YOU'RE STILL RATHER YOUNG AND NEW AT THIS GAME AREN'T YOU, COLIN?
Claret
YOU SEE, CHRISTMAS FREEBIES ARE A TOKEN OF THE ESTEEM IN WHICH ONE IS HELD BY CLIENTS THAT ONE HAS NURTURED AND DONE BUSINESS WITH IN THE COURSE OF ONE'S CAREER...
YOU'LL FIND THERE'S A DIRECT CORRELATION BETWEEN A PERSON'S EXPERIENCE AND LENGTH OF SERVICE IN THE CITY AND THE QUALITY AND AMOUNT OF COMPLIMENTARY BOOZE YOU'LL SEE HIM RECEIVING AT THIS TIME OF YEAR...
LOOK AT MY OWN DESK FOR EXAMPLE...
ER... BUT YOU HAVEN'T GOT ANY AT ALL, ALEX.
EXACTLY. I HAVE THE SENSE TO GET MY LOT DELIVERED AT HOME TO AVOID HAVING TO SHARE IT OUT...
WINE
WINE
NICE STUFF. I'LL HAVE SOME OF THIS...

Alex
PEATTIE + TAYLOR
YOU'LL HAVE TO UNDERSTAND SOMETHING OF THE WORKINGS OF THE STOCK MARKET, BRIDGET... THERE'S A SAYING IN THE CITY: "THE PRICE IS IN THE MARKET..."
WHAT THIS MEANS IS THAT ONE ACTS IN ADVANCE OF ANTICIPATED EVENTS... THE CONFIDENT EXPECTATION OF THEM WILL BE ENOUGH TO TRIGGER OFF THE APPROPRIATE FINANCIAL RESPONSE...
email: alex-cartoon@etgate.co.uk
SO THAT WHEN, SAY, A PIECE OF POSITIVE NEWS ACTUALLY MATERIALISES THERE WILL NOT BE THE FLURRY OF BUYING THAT YOU MIGHT EXPECT BECAUSE THAT BUYING WILL ALREADY HAVE BEEN DONE...
LET ME GET THIS CLEAR, CLIVE...
THIS BONUS CHEQUE... YOU'VE ALREADY SPENT IT...
THAT'S JUST IT... IT PRECISELY MATCHES THE OVERDRAFT I'VE BUILT UP SINCE SEPTEMBER...
YOU ARE DEAD, YOU REALISE...

Alex
PEATTIE + TAYLOR
AND THAT FIRST CHRISTMAS THE THREE KINGS CAME TO THE LOWLY-BORN MESSIAH BEARING GIFTS OF GOLD, FRANKINCENSE AND MYRRH..
BIBLE STORIES
NOW THESE MIGHT NOT SOUND LIKE VERY SUITABLE GIFTS FOR A BABY BUT THERE WAS A REASON FOR THESE PRESENTS...
THEY WERE ABOUT THE SYMBOLISING OF VALUE... THE REAL MEANING OF SUCH GIFTS WAS NOT MEANT TO BE APPRECIATED UNTIL LATER...
NOD
email: alex-cartoon@etgate.co.uk
I SEE... THEY GAVE US RECEIPTS SO WE CAN TAKE THEM BACK TO THE SHOP?
WOW! LOOK HOW MUCH THIS COST!
ZZZZ..

BONUS CHEQUE

Alex
PEATTIE+TAYLOR
WELL THE BROKERS HAVE ORGANISED AN OFFICE SWEEPSTAKE. EACH OF THEM HAS PICKED THE SHARE THEY THINK WILL GO UP THE MOST IN THE NEXT TWELVE MONTHS...
ALL THE BROKERS ARE DOING IT, EH?
YES, THEY PUT ¥20 NOTES IN A KITTY AND AT THE END OF 1997 WHOEVER'S SHARE TIP WAS MOST SUCCESSFUL WILL COLLECT ALL THE MONEY. IT'S JUST A HARMLESS BIT OF FUN, GERRY...
BUT I GUESS YOU COULD SAY THAT IF THEY'RE PREPARED TO PUT ¥20 OF THEIR OWN CASH TO BACK THEIR JUDGEMENT THEN THAT SAYS SOMETHING ABOUT THEM EACH HAVING SELF-CONFIDENCE IN THEIR OWN ACUMEN DOESN'T IT?
I GUESS SO...
email: alex-cartoon@etgate.co.uk
SO NONE OF THEM EXPECT TO BE HEADHUNTED OFF TO ANOTHER JOB BEFORE THE END OF THE YEAR.
DEPRESSING ISN'T IT? WHAT A BUNCH OF LOSERS.

Alex
PEATTIE + TAYLOR
FANCY A SPOT OF LUNCH, ALEX? YOU CAN TELL ME ALL ABOUT YOUR HOLIDAY IN ANGUILLA...
LUNCH? NO THANKS, CLIVE... ACTUALLY I THINK I'LL JOIN THE JANUARY HERDS DOWN AT THE GYM...
YOU MUST BE MAD...
email: alex-cartoon@etgate.co.uk
CONSIDER, CLIVE, I'VE SPENT THE LAST TWO WEEKS LAZING AROUND ON A TROPICAL BEACH EATING AND DRINKING MYSELF STUPID IN INDULGENT LUXURY...
SO YOU WANT TO WORK OFF THAT FAT?
ER... NO... I JUST CAN'T THINK OF ANY OTHER CROWDED PLACE WHERE I CAN WEAR THIS T-SHIRT...
EXCELSIOR HOTEL
ANGUILLA

CHETWYNDS CITY GYM AND HEALTH CLUB
EXCELSIOR HOTEL

Alex
BEATTIE + TAYLOR
THE THING ABOUT CHRISTMAS IS YOU TAKE ALL THIS TROUBLE TO GO OUT AND BUY THESE REALLY WONDERFUL EXPENSIVE PRESENTS FOR YOUR CHILDREN... THEN YOU WONDER IF ALL YOUR EFFORTS ARE A WASTE...
I MEAN, LIKE CHRISTOPHER'S REACTION WHEN HE OPENED HIS PRESENT: TO BE HONEST, HE JUST SHRUGGED SULKILY AS IF HE JUST TOOK IT FOR GRANTED...
YOU KNOW I REALLY COULDN'T TELL IF HE LIKED IT OR NOT OR WHAT HE THOUGHT OF IT... HE MIGHT HAVE BEEN REALLY DISAPPOINTED FOR ALL WE COULD TELL...
GOSH
YOU MUST HAVE BEEN AWFULLY PROUD OF HIM...
YES, IF HE CAN BE LIKE THAT WHEN HE'S OLD ENOUGH TO BE GETTING HIS BONUS CHEQUE FROM HIS BOSS IT WILL STAND HIM IN VERY GOOD STEAD...
email: alex-cartoon@etgate.co.uk

Alex
BEATTIE + TAYLOR
WELL, THE EXCITEMENT OF XMAS BONUS ANNOUNCEMENTS IS OVER. EVERYONE'S COME BACK TO MISERABLE FREEZING WEATHER...
WE'VE GIVEN THEM HUGE SALES TARGETS BUT THEY CAN'T START DOING ANY BUSINESS BECAUSE ALL THEIR CLIENTS HAVE GIVEN UP DRINKING AND DON'T WANT TO GO OUT TO LUNCH...
PLUS THEY'VE ALL GIVEN UP DRINKING TOO, SO THEY'RE ALL IN FILTHY STROPPY MOODS, JUST BITCHING AND SNAPPING AT ONE ANOTHER...
BUT LOOK AT PARSONS: THE CALM AT THE CENTRE OF THE STORM, COOL, CONTROLLED, UNFLAPPABLE, REFUSES TO BE RILED OR PROVOKED... IT SAYS A LOT ABOUT HIM...
YES...
...THAT HE'S GOT A NEW JOB LINED UP FOR AS SOON AS HE'S BANKED HIS BONUS AND HE DOESN'T WANT TO RISK DOING ANYTHING TO PREJUDICE ITS PAYMENT...
SNEAKY LITTLE RAT. WE'VE GOT HIM MARKED...

Alex
BEATTIE + TAYLOR
GYM
SO THIS IS THE GUY WHO WANTS A COMPLETE PHYSICAL MAKEOVER... LET'S HAVE A LOOK AT HIM.
HOLY COW.
WHAT A WEEDY FELLOW... SKINNY ARMS, SPARROW LEGS, PENCIL NECK, NO BICEPS, NO ABS...
WHAT ARE WE GOING TO DO WITH YOU?
I GUESS WE SHOULD START WITH HIS PECS...
YEAH, THEY'RE HOPELESS...
OKAY...
email: alex-cartoon@etgate.co.uk
SO YOU THINK I SHOULD WEAR CONTACT LENSES?
BLINK
BLINK

Alex
BEATTIE + TAYLOR
I CAN SEE YOU ARE VERY INEXPERIENCED IN DEALING WITH CITY PEOPLE... HAVE YOU NO UNDERSTANDING OR DISCRETION?
OBVIOUSLY I HAVE TO MAKE USE OF YOUR PROFESSIONAL SERVICES TO SECRETLY FIND MYSELF A NEW JOB. IN FUTURE PLEASE ALWAYS PHONE ME AT HOME...
IF YOU MUST CALL ME AT WORK AND ONE OF MY COLLEAGUES ANSWERS AND INFORMS YOU I'M OUT OF THE OFFICE, THEN JUST HANG UP OR SAY YOU'LL CALL BACK.
email: alex-cartoon@etgate.co.uk
KINDLY DO NOT ANNOUNCE YOUR NAME AND THE COMPANY YOU WORK FOR AND DO NOT STATE THE EXACT REASON OF YOUR CALL TO ME...
I JUST SAID IT WAS YOUR DENTAL SURGERY CONFIRMING YOUR APPOINTMENT FOR NEXT WEEK.
BUT I'D TOLD EVERYONE I WAS AT THE DENTIST'S WHEN I WAS IN FACT OUT SEEING MY HEADHUNTER...
SURGERY HOURS
BRUSH REGUL

Alex
PEATTIE + TAYLOR
SO, HERE'S MEGA-BANK'S OFFER TO YOU:- HEAD OF JAPANESE BOND TRADING. ¥700,000 P.A. PLUS GUARANTEED £1 M BONUS...
WOW... WHAT A PACKAGE!
DARWIN & THOMPSON EXECUTIVE RECRUITMENT
ECEPTION
email: alex-cartoon@etgate.co.uk
WELL, THE IDEA IS YOU'LL RACK UP COLOSSAL PROFITS FOR THEM. THOUGH OF COURSE IT IS TRUE THAT INTENSE COMPETITION HAS PUSHED UP CITY SALARIES TO STRATOSPHERIC LEVELS OF LATE...
YES... MAYBE...
...AND IT COULD BE ARGUED THAT THE INDIVIDUALS RESPONSIBLE ARE PEOPLE POSSESSED OF NO REAL SKILLS OTHER THAN A BIT OF MARKET NOUS AND PLENTY OF CHUTZPAH AND SALESMANSHIP...
WELL, I SUPPOSE SO.
...FUELLED BY NOTHING BUT PERSONAL GREED, BUT IN A FREE MARKET A PERSON SHOULD BE ENTITLED TO A SHARE OF WHAT HE MAKES FOR OTHERS...
YES... YES... OKAY...
THAT'S YOU ... WHAT ABOUT ME?
YOU'RE JUST A LUCKY LITTLE TINKER... BUT I'M ON 1/3 OF YOUR FIRST YEAR'S EARNINGS.

Alex
PEATTIE + TAYLOR
TYPICAL! YOU'RE HARDLY BACK FROM CHRISTMAS AND YOU'RE ALL BOOKING YOUR EASTER SKIING BREAKS AND SUMMER HOLIDAYS ALREADY...
SKI
HOLIDA 97
YOU SEEM TO HAVE NO PROBLEMS USING YOUR EMPLOYER'S TIME AND PHONE BILL FOR PERSONAL MATTERS... AM I THE ONLY PERSON GIVING ANY THOUGHT TO OUR CLIENTS AND THEIR NEEDS?
SKI
YOU SHOULD BE THINKING ABOUT GETTING OUT TO SEE THEM TO DISCUSS STRATEGY FOR THE YEAR AHEAD, VISITING POTENTIAL NEW CLIENT COMPANIES OR ACQUISITION TARGETS...
SKI
CAN WE GET OUR PRIORITIES RIGHT HERE..?
FIRST YOU SET UP A LOAD OF SPURIOUS BUSINESS TRIPS AND THEN, USING THE RESULTING AIR MILES, YOU CAN BOOK YOURSELF AN EXOTIC VACATION...
SKI
THANKYOU...

Alex
PEATTIE + TAYLOR
DON'T GET TOO EXCITED, FLETCHER. IT'S ONLY A MOBILE PHONE WE'VE GIVEN YOU. EVEN A GRADUATE TRAINEE NEEDS ONE.
YES, BUT THIS IS A SIGN THAT I'M FINALLY ADVANCING IN THE BANK.
I DIDN'T JOIN THE CITY TO BE A GENERAL OFFICE DOGSBODY... THIS IS HOW I'D IMAGINED MYSELF: ENTRUSTED WITH CONDUCTING A VITAL TRANSACTION FOR THE ORGANISATION, RECEIVING LAST MINUTE INSTRUCTIONS FROM MY COLLEAGUES ON THIS.
ER...YES, FLETCHER.
IT'S NOT SO UNTHINKABLE, IS IT? I MEAN, THERE'S A NATURAL ORDER BUT, FOR EXAMPLE, PEOPLE'S ROLES CAN CHANGE WITHIN IT CAN'T THEY?
OF COURSE THEY CAN...
FLETCHER... ABOUT MY ORDER: I'D LIKE TO CHANGE MY ROLL FROM A GRANARY TO A PLAIN WHITE BAP PLEASE...
ER... OKAY, ALEX.
SAND WICHES
TUNA

Alex
PEATTIE + TAYLOR
ANYTHING ELSE, GENTLEMEN?
ER...
ER...
HANG ON GUYS... IT'S 1-50... ISN'T IT TIME WE OUGHT TO BE GETTING BACK TO THE OFFICE?
REMEMBER THE NEW RULES ABOUT NOT TAKING LONG LUNCHES? THEY'RE AMAZINGLY STRICT NOW AND ANYTHING UNTOWARDS IS GOING TO GET NOTICED...
MAYBE WE SHOULD BE TAKING THAT INTO ACCOUNT BEFORE WE THINK OF INDULGING IN OUR USUAL 4-HOUR LUNCHEON...
ACTUALLY I THINK WE'D LIKE TO PAY OUR BILL NOW PLEASE, GERARD.
YES SIR...
AND STICK 3 DESSERTS, THE CHEESEBOARD, NINE BRANDIES AND A COUPLE MORE BOTTLES OF POUILLY-FUME ON IT IN ADVANCE... THAT SHOULD SEE US THROUGH TILL 3-30ISH...
OF COURSE.
YES. ACCOUNTS ARE BOUND TO CHECK THE "TIME PAID" ON OUR ITEMISED BILL WHEN WE SUBMIT IT ON EXPENSES...

Alex
PEATTIE + TAYLOR
ALEX, I HOPE YOU'LL BE SWITCHING YOUR MOBILE PHONE OFF FOR THE PERFORMANCE.
OF COURSE I WILL, PENNY.
OPERA HOUSE BAR
BUT I AM EXPECTING RATHER AN URGENT CALL FROM A CLIENT, SO I'M USING THE "CALL DIVERT" FUNCTION TO AUTOMATICALLY ROUTE ALL INCOMING CALLS THROUGH TO ANOTHER NUMBER WHICH I CAN PROGRAM IN...
PLICK
PLICK
THUS SPARING ME THE EMBARRASSMENT AND SOCIAL STIGMA OF MY PHONE RINGING IN THE MIDDLE OF THE OPERA, YET STILL ENABLING MY CLIENT TO GET A MESSAGE THROUGH TO ME...
PLICK
PLICK
email: alex-cartoon@etgate.co.uk
RING RING
I PROGRAMMED IN CLIVE'S MOBILE NUMBER... I'D BETTER SLIP OUT AND GIVE MY CLIENT A RING IN CASE IT WAS HIM TRYING TO REACH ME...

Alex
BEATTIE + TAYLOR
SO BASICALLY YOUR CAREER PLANS UNDER A LABOUR GOVERNMENT REMAIN THE SAME AS THEY'VE ALWAYS BEEN...?
ABSOLUTELY. I'M NOT WORRIED BY ALL THAT "RED MENACE" SCAREMONGERING...
I FEEL ASSURED THAT A NEW "SOCIALIST" ADMINISTRATION WILL WANT TO KEEP THINGS PRETTY MUCH AS THEY ARE FOR THE BUSINESS COMMUNITY...
I THINK THEY REALISE THE IMPORTANCE OF THE MARKET AND WON'T MAKE TOO MANY DRASTIC FUNDAMENTAL ECONOMIC CHANGES TO IT... WEALTH CREATION AND ENTERPRISE WILL STILL BE THE ORDER OF THE DAY...
RIGHT...
SO THAT'S HONG KONG UNDER CHINESE RULE... AND YOU'D STILL PLAN TO APPLY FOR A JOB THERE IF THE TORIES LOSE?
BLOODY RIGHT... SAME AS IN THE LAST ELECTION.. THIS COUNTRY WILL BE GOING TO THE DOGS IF THOSE BLAIRITE PINKOS GET POWER...

ZZZZ...
NEWS
HORLICK
HORLICK THIS
HORLICK THAT
HORLICK
OVAL-TINE

Alex
PEATTIE + TAYLOR
SO YOU HEAD UP A TEAM OF FUND MANAGERS BUT YOU'RE ALSO A MOTHER TO 5 KIDS..?
IT'S A REAL BALLANCING ACT, CLIVE...
AND I'VE OFTEN WORRIED IF I'M DOING THE RIGHT THING... I WORRY ABOUT THEM MISSING ME WHEN I'M NOT THERE...THERE'S SO MUCH PRESSURE ON ONE TO JUST STAY WITH THEM FULL TIME AND PEOPLE CAN BE SO JUDGEMENTAL IF ONE ISN'T...
OBVIOUSLY I GET TERRIBLY ANXIOUS ABOUT HOW IT AFFECTS THEM AND HOW THEY COPE WHEN I'M FORCED TO BE AWAY FROM THEM SO MUCH...
LIKE WHEN YOU'RE ON MATERNITY LEAVE? YES, WHAT IF THEY MANAGE THE FUNDS PERFECTLY WELL IN YOUR ABSENCE?
EXACTLY. MY BOSS MIGHT DECIDE I'M NOT WORTH MY MILLION QUID BONUS.

Alex
PEATTIE + TAYLOR
THE SO- CALLED FUNDAMENTALISTS ARGUE THAT THE ONLY GUIDING PRINCIPLE TO INVESTMENT SHOULD BE THE UNIQUE ECONOMIC FACTORS THAT PERTAIN AT THE MOMENT...
BUT AS FUND MANAGERS WE WOULD BE FOOLISH TO IGNORE THE OTHER APPROACH, NAMELY STUDYING TABLES OF PAST STOCK MARKET TRENDS AND LOOKING FOR SIGNIFICANT CORRELATIONS...
email: alex-cartoon@etgate.co.uk
TAKE 1987... NOTE HOW THE YEAR BEGAN, LIKE THIS YEAR, ON A RECORD HIGH. YET IN OCTOBER PRICES PLUMMET OVER-NIGHT LOSING 25% OF THEIR VALUE... WHAT SHOULD THIS TELL US ABOUT OUR STRATEGY TOWARDS THE END OF THE YEAR?
1987
WELL SOMETIME IN LATE AUTUMN WE COULD ISSUE FIGURES SHOWING HOW MUCH OUR FUND HAS GONE UP IN A TEN-YEAR PERIOD I.E.:- STARTING RIGHT HERE AFTER THE CRASH...
1987
OCT NOV DEC
YES. EVEN WE COULDN'T FAIL TO LOOK GOOD BY THAT CRITERION...

Alex
PEATTIE + TAYLOR
I MUST SAY I DIDN'T THINK STUART WOULD MAKE IT INTO WORK TODAY...
ME NEITHER. APPARENTLY HE WAS ON A HUGE BENDER TILL 4.30 AM...
TEA
COFFEE
WHEN HIS ALARM CLOCK RANG A SCANT HOUR AFTER HE HAD STUMBLED INTO BED HE MUST HAVE BEEN HUGELY TEMPTED TO TAKE THE DAY OFF...
TEA
COFFEE
BUT THAT WOULD HAVE BEEN CONTRARY TO THE SPIRIT AND TRADITION OF THE CITY...
email: alex-cartoon@etgate.co.uk
EXACTLY. NO MATTER HOW RAVAGED YOUR BODY MAY BE BY THE EFFECTS OF ALCOHOL AND LACK OF SLEEP IT'S A MATTER OF PRINCIPLE AND PRIDE TO HAUL YOURSELF OUT OF BED AND ONTO THE TRAIN...
...AND SLEEP OFF YOUR HANGOVER ON THE COMPANY'S TIME...
JUST LOOK AT HIM... A SHINING EXAMPLE TO US ALL...
ZZZZ...

Alex
BEATTIE + TAYLOR
SO WILL YOU BE CANVASSING ON BEHALF OF THE CONSERVATIVES THIS ELECTION?
AS A BASIC BELIEVER IN CAPITALISM AND THE MARKET ECONOMY I BELIEVE I DO HAVE A DUTY, CLIVE...
IT'S NOT LIKE THE LAST ELECTION...THE ECONOMY IS BASICALLY PERFORMING WELL AT THE MOMENT, EXPORTS ARE BUOYANT, COMPANIES ARE EXPANDING AND OPTIMISTIC... BUT THIS MESSAGE HAS NOT FILTERED THROUGH TO THE MAN IN THE STREET...
YES. LABOUR IS WAY AHEAD IN THE POLLS...
EXACTLY. AND PEOPLE LIKE ME WHO ACTUALLY UNDERSTAND WHAT'S HAPPENING IN THE COUNTRY CAN'T JUST BE PASSIVE ABOUT IT IN THE RUN UP TO POLLING DAY...
email: alex-cartoon@etgate.co.uk
OUR CLIENT COMPANIES ARE ALL IN THE MONEY AND NEED US TO DO ALL THESE LUCRATIVE LAST MINUTE DEALS FOR THEM BEFORE THE ELECTION DEADLINE AND NEW LABOUR'S KILLJOY CORPORATION LAWS...
I'VE TOLD MY LOCAL CONSERVATIVE ASSOCIATION TO GET STUFFED... I SHALL BE FAR TOO BUSY.

Alex
PEATTIE + TAYLOR
SO THEY'VE EXTENDED THE INFAMOUS ANTI-TERRORIST "RING OF PLASTIC"
THAT'S RIGHT, CLIVE. MOST OF THE STREETS IN THE SQUARE MILE SEEM TO BE BLOCKED OFF NOW.
TO THE AVERAGE CITY PERSON IT JUST BRINGS THE IRRITATION AND DISRUPTION OF EVEN MORE TRAFFIC CONGESTION, BUT I SUPPOSE ANY MEASURE WHICH HAS EVEN AN OUTSIDE CHANCE OF FOILING CRIMINAL INTENTIONS IS FOR THE GOOD...
TAXI
OF COURSE IT SEEMS UNLIKELY THAT ANY POTENTIAL WRONGDOER ENGAGED IN AN ORCHESTRATED CAMPAIGN OF SUBVERSION WOULD BE STUPID ENOUGH TO GET CAUGHT IN SUCH AN OBVIOUS TRAP BUT SOME OF THEM ARE YOUNG AND INEXPERIENCED...
NOW, PHILLIPS, YOU'VE SUBMITTED AN EXPENSES CLAIM FOR £5 FOR A TAXI TO A MEETING AT METROBANK LAST WEEK... YET WITH THIS EXTRA CONGESTION THE JOURNEY SHOULD HAVE COST AT LEAST £9...
ADMIT IT... YOU WALKED AND FAKED THIS RECEIPT...
ER...

Alex
AH... MY BLEEP'S GONE OFF... THIS IS THE NEW PAGER SERVICE WE'VE ALL GOT INSTEAD OF HAVING IRKSOME MOBILE PHONE INTERRUPTIONS.
BLEEP BLEEP...
OH... IT'S A MESSAGE FOR MICHAEL.
THE SYSTEM IS DESIGNED SO THAT IF A CLIENT PHONES FOR ONE INDIVIDUAL THE MESSAGE IS PAGED TO EVERYONE ELSE FROM THE SAME OFFICE TO ENSURE THAT SOMEONE ELSE WILL RETURN THE CALL IF THE INTENDED RECIPIENT IS UNAVAILABLE...
IN OTHER WORDS, IF MICHAEL IS UNABLE TO RESPOND THEN WE, HIS COLLEAGUES, WILL RECEIVE THE MESSAGE MEANT FOR HIM AND CAN TAKE APPROPRIATE ACTION...
YES... LET'S SEE...
COVER HIM IN LIPSTICK TO GET HIM IN EVEN WORSE TROUBLE?
YES... THAT'S THE THIRD TIME HIS WIFE HAS CALLED THIS EVENING...
BLEEP BLEEP BLEEP
Michael. Where the hell are you? Joan.

Alex
PEATTIE+TAYLOR
WHAT?! OUR BOSS HAS RESIGNED?..
WELL, IT'S HARDLY SURPRISING TIMING IS IT? AFTER ALL, EVERYONE'S BONUSES WERE PAID OUT 3 DAYS AGO...
I IMAGINE HE WAITED FOR THE CHEQUE TO CLEAR, THEN WENT IN TO THE CHAIRMAN AND TOLD HIM HE WAS OFF TO ANOTHER JOB...
HE'S RUN THIS DEPARTMENT FOR FIVE YEARS... AND NOW HE'S GONE? JUST LIKE THAT?
email: alex-cartoon@etgate.co.uk
I FEEL TOTALLY POLEAXED... JUST NUMB AND EMPTY... I'M OVERWHELMED BY A HUGE SENSE OF LOSS AND REGRET AND DESPAIR...
I'M SORRY, OLD CHAP. WE ALL KNOW WHAT YOU THOUGHT OF HIM...
PAT PAT
...THAT HE WAS A TOTAL OLD S-H-ONE-T...
EXACTLY. AND I WAS SO LOOKING FORWARD TO TELLING HIM SO TO HIS FACE LATER THIS AFTERNOON WHEN I PLAN TO HAND IN MY RESIGNATION.
DAMN... DAMN...

Alex
BEATTIE + TAYLOR
I'M GOING TO "BUFF'S" ON FRIDAY.
THAT PUB WHERE GIRLS STRIP OFF FOR THE LUNCHTIME CLIENTELLE. WHY?
DIARY
WELL I HOPE THIS DOESN'T SOUND PRETENTIOUS, ALEX, BUT HAVE YOU EVER CONSIDERED THAT THE CLOTHES WE WEAR ARE BASICALLY ABOUT SOCIAL CONTROL OVER ONE'S BEHAVIOUR FROM WHICH WE ALL YEARN SOMETIMES TO BE LIBERATED...
AND IT'S ONLY IN THE CONTEXT OF CERTAIN INSTITUTIONS THAT PRESENT THE SPECTACLE OF INDIVIDUALS DIVESTING THEMSELVES OF SUCH GARMENTS THAT ONE CAN DISCOVER IN ONESELF THE EXPERIENCE OF A LESS OPPRESSED LEVEL OF CONSCIOUSNESS...
I KNOW WHAT YOU'RE TALKING ABOUT, CLIVE...
...BUT I STILL THINK IT'S A RATHER HIGH-FALUTING WAY OF DESCRIBING CASUAL DRESS DAY.
SINCE I WON'T HAVE TO WEAR A TIE ON FRIDAY I CAN SIT RIGHT AT THE FRONT AND NOT WORRY ABOUT HAVING IT MISTREATED BY THE ARTISTES...
BETTER LEAVE YOUR SPECS OFF TOO.

Alex
PEATTIE + TAYLOR
ALEX, THERE'S THIS NEW OFFER TO READERS OF SOME NEWSPAPERS:- IF YOU GO TO CERTAIN RESTAURANTS YOU CAN GET SPECIAL CUT-PRICE MEALS FOR A FIVER AT THE MOMENT.
REALLY?
THIS COULD BE A VERY GOOD WAY OF DINING MY CLIENTS CHEAPLY... IMAGINE: I COULD COME BACK FROM LUNCH LESS THAN 20 QUID OUT OF POCKET... THAT'S THE WAY TO STAY SOLVENT!
INDEEDY!
BUT DON'T FORGET TO BRING ALONG THE ALL-IMPORTANT LITTLE SLIP OF PAPER THAT HAS TO BE PRESENTED...
OH... IS THERE A COUPON? WHERE?
NO NO NO... A BLANK RECEIPT FROM THE RESTAURANT... YOU ARE GOING TO CLAIM YOUR NORMAL EXORBITANT EXPENSES FOR A CLIENT LUNCH, AREN'T YOU?
GOOD GRIEF. MUST I TELL YOU EVERYTHING?

Alex
PEATTIE + TAYLOR
HERE YOU ARE... ONE BACON AND AVOCADO ON BROWN...
THANKS, DAVIES.
THE SANDWICH BOX
IS THAT REALLY FOR YOU, MISTER LONG-LUNCH?
I'M ADAPTING TO CIRCUMSTANCES THAT'S ALL, MIKE. WE'RE IN A FIERCELY COMPETITIVE BUSINESS ENVIRONMENT THESE DAYS... I'VE HAD TO CHANGE MY HABITS SOMEWHAT...
UNWRAP
I MEAN, THE OLD DAYS WHEN ONE COULD JUST SKIVE OFF TO LUNCH FOR THREE HOURS LEAVING A JACKET ON THE BACK OF ONE'S CHAIR ARE WELL OVER...
MUNCH
email: alex.cartoon@etgate.co.uk
NOWADAYS YOU HAVE TO LEAVE A SANDWICH WITH A BITE TAKEN OUT OF IT ON YOUR DESK AS WELL... FOR ADDED AUTHENTICITY...
RIGHT. I'M OFF.

Alex
PEATTIE + TAYLOR
WITH SO MUCH POACHING OF ENTIRE TEAMS AROUND I'M GLAD WE FOLLOWED THE LEAD OF OTHER BANKS AND HIRED THE SERVICES OF A PRIVATE DETECTIVE...
GLAD TO BE OF ASSISTANCE, SIR.
MEGABANK HEAD OF INVESTMENT BANKING
I'D SUSPECTED THAT OONA CRICKHILL AND HER TEAM WERE PLOTTING SOMETHING DEVIOUS... SO THIS IS A TAPE YOU SECRETLY MADE OF THEM ACTUALLY DISCUSSING THEIR PROPOSED DEFECTION IN A LOCAL WINE BAR?
THAT'S RIGHT...
THANK YOU. WHEN A NO-HOLDS-BARRED BIDDING WAR IS ABOUT TO COMMENCE IT STRENGTHENS OUR HAND TO HAVE AN ADVANCE IDEA OF THE SORT OF SALARY LEVELS BEING TALKED ABOUT...
email: alex-cartoon@etgate.co.uk
...WE ONLY EARN ¥50,000 AT OUR PRESENT JOBS BUT WE'LL SCAM THAT OLD CODGER AT MEGABANK THAT WE'RE ON ¥75,000 EACH...
AHEM... SO, SHALL WE START AT 60K...?

Alex
BEATTIE + TAYLOR
BRIDGET, ABOUT FRIDAY. YOU KNOW WHAT IT'S ALWAYS LIKE ON VALENTINE'S DAY:- IMPOSSIBLE TO GET A RESERVATION, ONE ENDS UP BEING OVERCHARGED FOR AN INDIFFERENT MEAL IN AN OVERCROWDED RESTAURANT...
LOOK, WHAT SAY WE FORGET TRYING TO GO OUT ON THE DAY ITSELF THIS YEAR AND HAVE OURSELVES A NICE COSY ROMANTIC MEAL OUT NEXT WEEK SOME TIME WHEN IT'S QUIETER?
THAT'S A CONSIDERATE THOUGHT, CLIVE...
email: alex-cartoon@etgate.co.uk
BUT, DON'T WORRY. APPARENTLY THERE'S A BIG RUGBY MATCH OVER IN IRELAND ON SATURDAY THAT ALL THE BOYS ARE FLYING OUT ON FRIDAY NIGHT FOR, SO IT SHOULD BE PRETTY MUCH DESERTED IN TOWN THAT EVENING...
PROBLEM, CLIVE?
ER...
BA DUBLIN

Alex
PEATTIE + TAYLOR
BLASTED HOLIDAY ARRANGEMENTS! I'M OFF TOMORROW AND AS USUAL I'VE LEFT EVERYTHING TILL THE LAST MINUTE...
OBVIOUSLY ONE WANTS TO GET A FINANCIALLY ADVANTAGEOUS DEAL IF POSSIBLE WHICH INVOLVES PHONING ROUND ALL THE COMPANIES... AND MOST OF THEM ARE TOTALLY UNHELPFUL...
BUT, ALEX, SURELY...
HERE ON YOUR DESK: A FULLY-BOOKED TWO-WEEK TROUT-FISHING HOLIDAY IN ARGENTINA WITH AIR TICKETS, CONNECTIONS, HOTEL RESERVATIONS, TRAVEL INSURANCE...
DON'T BE DENSE, CLIVE...
Holiday Tours
I'M PHONING ROUND OUR CLIENTS TO SEE IF ANY OF THEM'S GOT A SUBSIDUARY OUT THERE I COULD VALIDLY BE VISITING SO I CAN SCAM THE WHOLE THING ON MY EXPENSES.

Alex
PEATTIE + TAYLOR
WITH THE GROWTH OF THE DERIVATIVES MARKET IN RECENT YEARS WE'VE SEEN BANKS INCREASINGLY WORRIED ABOUT THE NICK-LEESON-TYPE SCENARIO WHILE SALARIES OF PEOPLE LIKE YOU AND ME HAVE GONE THROUGH THE ROOF...
NOW, THE BANK OF ENGLAND IS SUGGESTING "NEGATIVE BONUSES", LOWER SALARIES AND PENALTIES FOR TRADERS TAKING BAD GAMBLES... SO AS TO MAKE THEM MORE FINANCIALLY RESPONSIBLE... I THINK THE IDEA STINKS...
YES. ME TOO.
IF BANKS START TRYING TO RESTRAIN THE MARKET; CONTROL THE RISKS; MAKE THE WHOLE SYSTEM SAFE... IT'S BOUND TO HAVE A DELETERIOUS KNOCK-ON EFFECT...
QUITE.
email: alex-cartoon@etgate.co.uk
OUR COMPLIANCE OFFICER SALARIES MIGHT GET REDUCED BACK DOWN TO 1985 LEVELS...
THEY ONLY PAY US SO MUCH BECAUSE THEY'RE SCARED SH*TLESS...

Alex
© PEATTIE + TAYLOR
WE WERE ONE OF THE FIRST CITY BANKS WITH THE FORESIGHT AND VISION TO SET UP OFFICES IN THE EX-COMMUNIST BLOC - WARSAW, BUCHAREST AND SO ON...
...AND NOW WITHIN A FEW YEARS THOSE COUNTRIES COULD BE FULLY INTEGRATED INTO THE EUROPEAN COMMUNITY, WITH THEIR CAPITALS THRIVING MODERN BUSINESS CENTRES...
BUT I IMAGINE YOU'LL CONTINUE TO EXPAND YOUR OPERATION...
OH YES... PROBABLY INTO THE CENTRAL ASIAN FORMER SOVIET REPUBLICS: KAZAKHSTAN, TURKMENISTAN ETC... TO KEEP ONE'S COMPANY DYNAMIC, THRUSTING AND COMPETITIVE ONE MUST BE CONSTANTLY ROLLING BACK THE FRONTIERS OF THE BUSINESS WORLD...
AH YES...
GOT TO HAVE SOME GODFORSAKEN PROVINCIAL OUTPOST YOU TRANSFER ALL YOUR USELESS EXECUTIVES TO...
QUITE. GET THEM TO RESIGN RATHER THAN GO TO ALL THE EXPENSE OF SACKING THEM...
email: alex-cartoon@etgate.co.uk

EUROPE
NEW POSTING
PINS

Alex
PEATTIE + TAYLOR
I HAVE THIS SET OF GOLF CLUBS THAT MY WIFE SAYS I TREAT AS MY UTTER PRIDE AND JOY... AND IT'S TRUE, THEY WERE AN EXTRAVAGANT PURCHASE...
IN FLIGHT
BUT THE FACT IS THAT FOR SOMEONE LIKE ME WHO WANTS TO SPEND A LOT OF TIME PLAYING GOLF THEN A DECENT SET OF STICKS LIKE THAT IS AN INVESTMENT...
FOR EXAMPLE, LIKE NOW, THIS WEEKEND I'M INVITED TO THIS BUSINESS CONFERENCE IN THE BAHAMAS WHICH, AS IS OFTEN THE CASE, HAS BEEN ARRANGED NEXT TO AN EXCELLENT GOLF COURSE...THEREFORE MY CLUBS WILL BE INVALUABLE...
...I'VE LEFT THEM AT HOME AND TOTALLY ALLAYED MY WIFE'S SUSPICIONS ABOUT WHETHER I'M JUST GOING AWAY ON ANOTHER FREEBIE.
AND YOU'LL HIRE A PERFECTLY ADEQUATE SET WHEN YOU GET THERE AS USUAL?
QUITE.

Alex
PEATTIE + TAYLOR
OF COURSE ALL THESE ANALYST CHAPPIES ARE WORKING PRETTY HARD AT THE MOMENT BECAUSE THE EXTEL SURVEY IS COMING UP...
HEAD OF RESEARCH
THAT'S THE OCCASION WHEN THEIR CLIENTS, THE INVESTMENT MANAGERS, HAVE THE CHANCE TO RATE THE INDIVIDUAL ECONOMISTS ON THE QUALITY OF THE RESEARCH THEY PUT OUT...
AH, THE INCOMPARABLE SKILLS OF THE ANALYST...
A QUICK GLANCE OVER A SET OF FIGURES AND HIS AGILE HIGHLY-NUMERATE BRAIN WILL IMMEDIATELY EXTRACT THE SIGNIFICANT INFORMATION, DO SOME QUICK MENTAL ARITHMETIC AND DRAW THE RELEVANT CONCLUSIONS AS TO PERFORMANCE...
HILL, THIS EXPENSES CLAIM FOR LAST MONTH IS PITIFUL. KINDLY STOP WASTING YOUR TIME WRITING REPORTS AND JUST GET OUT THERE AND LUNCH EVERYONE WHO'S ELIGIBLE TO VOTE...

Alex
PEATTIE + TAYLOR
WELL, PRACTICALLY THE WHOLE OFFICE SEEMS TO HAVE DRESSED DOWN FOR "RED NOSE DAY" TODAY...
BUT NOT QUITE EVERYONE... TO THE ANNOYANCE OF CLIVE.
YOU SEE, CLIVE HAS ALWAYS BEEN A MOST PASSIONATE AND DEDICATED SUPPORTER OF COMIC RELIEF AND ALL THE GOOD CAUSES IT RAISES MONEY FOR...
AND IT REALLY MAKES HIS BLOOD BOIL WHEN HE COMES ACROSS INDIVIDUALS WHO THROUGH IGNORANCE, NARROW-MINDEDNESS OR AN UNCHARITABLE NATURE CAN'T BE RELIED UPON TO ENTER INTO THE SPIRIT OF TODAY'S EVENT...
LIKE THE PEOPLE HE'S GOT THAT SECRET JOB INTERVIEW WITH TODAY?
PRECISELY.
ACUTE SELF-CONSCIOUSNESS

Alex
PEATTIE + TAYLOR
BLESS ME FATHER FOR I HAVE SINNED... I THINK I MAY BE PREGNANT AND I'M NOT MARRIED...
TELL ME ABOUT IT MY CHILD.
email: alex-cartoon@etgate.co.uk
YOU'RE MY ONLY HOPE... YOU SEE I'VE HEARD THAT THE HOLY CHURCH IS OFFERING AID TO WOMEN IN FINANCIAL DIFFICULTIES TO GO AHEAD WITH THEIR PREGNANCIES... ...IS THAT TRUE...?
YES WE WILL GIVE WHATEVER HELP WE CAN...
I'M A HIGHLY PAID TRADER IN THE CITY, FATHER... HAVING A BABY AT THIS POINT IN MY CAREER WOULD BE A DISASTER FOR ME... IT WOULD BE SHAMEFUL AND I'D LOSE EVERYTHING... I DON'T KNOW WHICH WAY TO TURN...
AND YOU THINK NO-ONE UNDERSTANDS YOUR POSITION?
YES.
I HOPE SO ANYWAY... IT'S A £77 MILLION DODGY LONG DERIVATIVES POSITION AND THE ONLY WAY MY EMPLOYERS CAN FIND OUT ABOUT IT IS IF I DO SOMETHING CRAZY LIKE GO OFF ON MATERNITY LEAVE...
BUT COULD YOU BAIL ME OUT, DO YOU THINK?
FAITH! THAT'S A LOT OF MOOLAH!

Alex
PEATTIE + TAYLOR
WALLACE SAYS HE'S GOING TO THE DENTIST BUT HE'S ACTUALLY OFF TO SEE A RECRUITMENT CONSULTANT ABOUT A NEW JOB...
HOW DO YOU KNOW?
BECAUSE I'M HAVING HIM "REVERSE HEADHUNTED". I WANT TO GET RID OF HIM BUT SACKING HIM WOULD BE TOO EXPENSIVE, SO I'M SECRETLY EMPLOYING A HEADHUNTER TO FIND HIM A POSITION ELSEWHERE...
MOST HUMANE...
email: alex-cartoon@etgate.co.uk
A VERY PRACTICAL ARRANGEMENT, ALEX. IT SPARES MY OWN FEELINGS ABOUT DOING SOMETHING UNPLEASANT AND ALLOWS ME TO TREAT WITH ALL DUE COURTESY A PERSON WHOM I WOULD NOT WISH TO UPSET UNNECESSARILY...
THE CANDIDATE YOU'RE INTERVIEWING FOR WALLACE'S OLD JOB...?
EXACTLY. HE'S COMING IN IN 5 MINUTES... IT CAN BE EMBARRASSING FOR THE NEW CHAP IF HE BUMPS INTO HIS PREDECESSOR-TO-BE...

Alex
BEATTIE + TAYLOR
...I CAN HARDLY SLEEP FOR WORRYING ABOUT OUR BANK'S VULNERABILITY TO DERIVATIVES LOSSES...IT'S BEEN GIVING ME NIGHTMARES...
NONE OF OUR BOFFINS HAS EVER BEEN ABLE TO PUT ANYTHING LIKE A PROPER FIGURE ON THE EXTENT OF OUR DOWNSIDE RISK...IN SPITE OF ALL THEIR FANCY-SOUNDING MATHEMATICAL EQUATIONS...
THAT'S NOT TRUE.
OUR LATEST PROGRAMMING UTILISES A FORMULA WHICH TAKES ACCOUNT OF VOLATILITY AND CAN GIVE AN ASSESSMENT OF OUR EXPOSURE AT ANY TIME...
AH, RIGHT... IS IT "VEGA"?
YES.
VAGUER THAN EVER, DAMMIT.... WHAT DOES THE COMPUTER SAY AGAIN...?
ER..."PROBABLY SOMEWHERE ABOUT BETWEEN 4 AND 60 MILLION IN THE RED, ROUGHLY"...
OH ****!
ZZZZZ

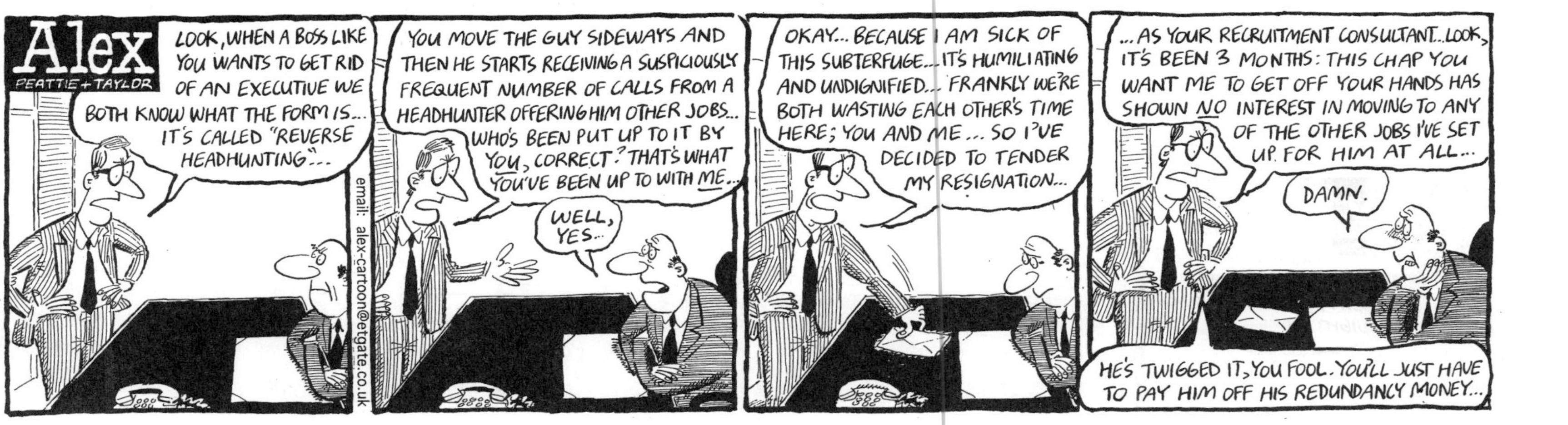
Alex
PEATTIE + TAYLOR
LOOK, WHEN A BOSS LIKE YOU WANTS TO GET RID OF AN EXECUTIVE WE BOTH KNOW WHAT THE FORM IS... IT'S CALLED "REVERSE HEADHUNTING"...
email: alex-cartoon@etgate.co.uk
YOU MOVE THE GUY SIDEWAYS AND THEN HE STARTS RECEIVING A SUSPICIOUSLY FREQUENT NUMBER OF CALLS FROM A HEADHUNTER OFFERING HIM OTHER JOBS... WHO'S BEEN PUT UP TO IT BY YOU, CORRECT? THAT'S WHAT YOU'VE BEEN UP TO WITH ME...
WELL, YES...
OKAY... BECAUSE I AM SICK OF THIS SUBTERFUGE... IT'S HUMILIATING AND UNDIGNIFIED... FRANKLY WE'RE BOTH WASTING EACH OTHER'S TIME HERE; YOU AND ME... SO I'VE DECIDED TO TENDER MY RESIGNATION...
...AS YOUR RECRUITMENT CONSULTANT... LOOK, IT'S BEEN 3 MONTHS: THIS CHAP YOU WANT ME TO GET OFF YOUR HANDS HAS SHOWN NO INTEREST IN MOVING TO ANY OF THE OTHER JOBS I'VE SET UP FOR HIM AT ALL...
DAMN.
HE'S TWIGGED IT, YOU FOOL. YOU'LL JUST HAVE TO PAY HIM OFF HIS REDUNDANCY MONEY...

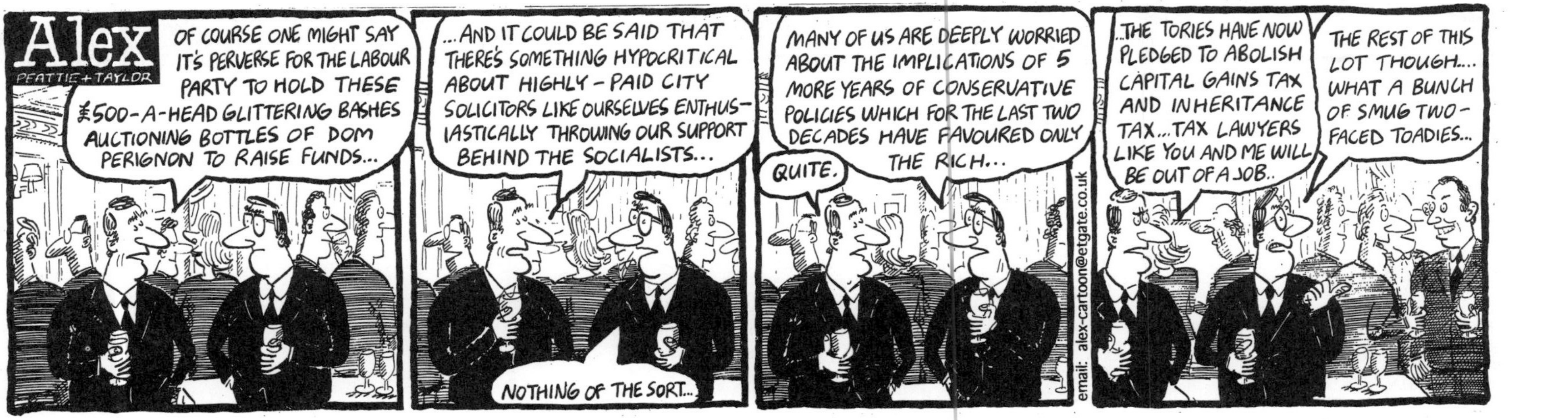
Alex
PEATTIE + TAYLOR
OF COURSE ONE MIGHT SAY IT'S PERVERSE FOR THE LABOUR PARTY TO HOLD THESE £500-A-HEAD GLITTERING BASHES AUCTIONING BOTTLES OF DOM PERIGNON TO RAISE FUNDS...
...AND IT COULD BE SAID THAT THERE'S SOMETHING HYPOCRITICAL ABOUT HIGHLY-PAID CITY SOLICITORS LIKE OURSELVES ENTHUSIASTICALLY THROWING OUR SUPPORT BEHIND THE SOCIALISTS...
NOTHING OF THE SORT...
MANY OF US ARE DEEPLY WORRIED ABOUT THE IMPLICATIONS OF 5 MORE YEARS OF CONSERVATIVE POLICIES WHICH FOR THE LAST TWO DECADES HAVE FAVOURED ONLY THE RICH...
QUITE.
email: alex-cartoon@etgate.co.uk
...THE TORIES HAVE NOW PLEDGED TO ABOLISH CAPITAL GAINS TAX AND INHERITANCE TAX... TAX LAWYERS LIKE YOU AND ME WILL BE OUT OF A JOB...
THE REST OF THIS LOT THOUGH... WHAT A BUNCH OF SMUG TWO-FACED TOADIES...

Alex
PEATTIE + TAYLOR
ONE DAY I SUPPOSE ALL JOB INTERVIEWS WILL BE DONE BY CANDIDATES GOING INTO THEIR LOCAL VIDEO-CONFERENCING BOOTH AND TALKING TO US BY VIDEO LINK.
OH I DON'T THINK SO...
email: alex-cartoon@etgate.co.uk
CALL ME OLD-FASHIONED BUT I'VE GOT A STUDENT COMING UP FROM CAMBRIDGE FOR AN INTERVIEW TODAY AND I WOULDN'T DREAM OF INTERVIEWING HIM BY VIDEOLINK...
I STILL BELIEVE THAT THE EFFECTIVE WAY FOR A PROSPECTIVE GRADUATE TRAINEE IN HIS CIRCUMSTANCES TO GIVE A PROPER IMPRESSION OF WHAT CALIBRE OF CHAP HE IS, IS BY COMING TO THE BANK IN PERSON...
IE:- CONSPICUOUSLY STANDING ON CAMBRIDGE RAILWAY STATION WEARING A SUIT, OBVIOUSLY OFF TO A JOB INTERVIEW, IN FULL VIEW OF HIS FELLOW STUDENTS AND TWO MONTHS AFTER EVERYONE ELSE GOT THEIR MILK-ROUND JOBS... HA HA... WHAT A LOSER!
YOU REALLY ARE A SADIST, ALEX.

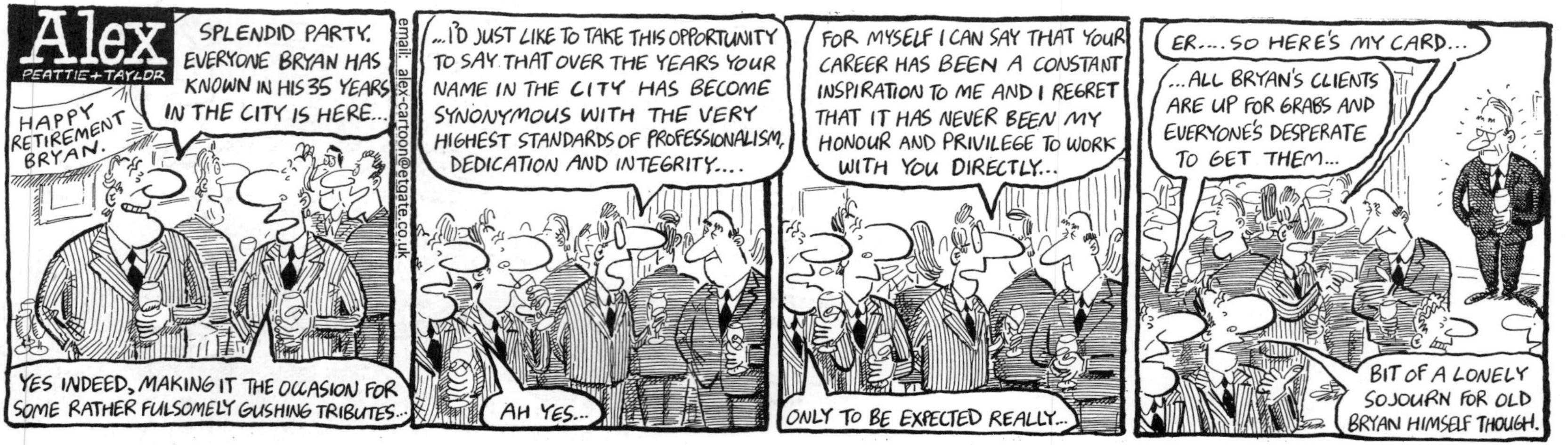
Alex
PEATTIE + TAYLOR
SPLENDID PARTY. EVERYONE BRYAN HAS KNOWN IN HIS 35 YEARS IN THE CITY IS HERE...
HAPPY RETIREMENT BRYAN.
YES INDEED, MAKING IT THE OCCASION FOR SOME RATHER FULSOMELY GUSHING TRIBUTES...
email: alex-cartoon@etgate.co.uk
...I'D JUST LIKE TO TAKE THIS OPPORTUNITY TO SAY THAT OVER THE YEARS YOUR NAME IN THE CITY HAS BECOME SYNONYMOUS WITH THE VERY HIGHEST STANDARDS OF PROFESSIONALISM, DEDICATION AND INTEGRITY....
AH YES...
FOR MYSELF I CAN SAY THAT YOUR CAREER HAS BEEN A CONSTANT INSPIRATION TO ME AND I REGRET THAT IT HAS NEVER BEEN MY HONOUR AND PRIVILEGE TO WORK WITH YOU DIRECTLY...
ONLY TO BE EXPECTED REALLY...
ER.... SO HERE'S MY CARD...
...ALL BRYAN'S CLIENTS ARE UP FOR GRABS AND EVERYONE'S DESPERATE TO GET THEM...
BIT OF A LONELY SOJOURN FOR OLD BRYAN HIMSELF THOUGH.

Alex
PEATTIE + TAYLOR
LIKE ALL BANKS WE'RE VERY WORRIED ABOUT OUR VULNERABILITY TO A HUGE DERIVATIVES LOSS. THE PROBLEM IS THE FIELD IS VERY HARD TO COMPREHEND.
email: alex-cartoon@etgate.co.uk
WE'VE TRIED ATTENDING RISK MANAGEMENT COURSES... WE'VE LOOKED AT VARIOUS SOFTWARE PACKAGES DESIGNED TO VALUE DERIVATIVE POSITIONS, BUT THEY ALL TEND TO SHOW CONTRADICTING RESULTS...
THE MOST IMPORTANT FORMULA IN THE PROGRAM IS "VEGA" THOUGH EVEN THAT IS NOT 100% RELIABLE...
RIGHT BUT WHEN WE'RE CONSIDERING THE CAPACITY OF ABSTRACT FORMULAS TO GIVE US MODELS OF RISK ASSESSMENT WE OUGHT FIRST OF ALL TO BE LOOKING AT VEGA'S ?
YES.
LAS VEGAS
BAR
LUCK
CASINO
FRUIT MACHINE
BANDIT
I THINK I BEGIN TO UNDERSTAND... SO, LIKE IT'S ALL A TOTAL FREE-FOR-ALL INCOMPREHENSIBLE HIGH-RISK ARBITRARY GAMBLE...?
YES. ACCEPT IT... IT'S THE ONLY WAY...

WHIRR
WHIRR...
DERIVATIVES
DERIV-ATIVES
DERIV-ATIVES
ZZZZ...

Alex
BEATTIE + TAYLOR
YOU SHOULD HAVE SEEN ALEX'S REACTION WHEN I TOLD HIM THAT HIS BRAND-NEW CAR HAD JUST BEEN MINDLESSLY VANDALISED BY YOUNG THUGS ON THE STREET OUTSIDE...
email: alex-cartoon@etgate.co.uk
WHAT IS IT THAT MODERN SOCIETY HAS DONE TO BRING UP A GENERATION THAT HAS COMPLETE DISRESPECT AND CONTEMPT FOR PROPERTY BELONGING TO OTHER PEOPLE?
IT SICKENS ME TO SEE IT...
THEY PERCEIVE THAT THE OWNER OF THE CAR IS MUCH RICHER THAN THEMSELVES AND THIS SEEMS TO VINDICATE THEIR CYNICAL AND PROFOUNDLY ANTI-SOCIAL ATTITUDE.
THANK GOODNESS THE GOVERNMENT IS SLOWLY TAKING ACTION TO STAMP IT OUT...
...IE:- PHASING OUT COMPANY CARS...
I MEAN LOOK AT ALEX. HE SIMPLY DOESN'T GIVE A DAMN. HE KNOWS THE BANK WILL SORT OUT ALL THE REPAIRS...

Alex
PEATTIE + TAYLOR
JULIAN'S STANDING AS A CONSERVATIVE CANDIDATE IN THE ELECTION. HE'S BACK TO UPDATE THE CHAPS ON HIS EXPERIENCES FROM THE CAMPAIGN TRAIL...
IT'S A REAL UPHILL STRUGGLE...THERE'S NEVER BEEN A RUN-UP TO AN ELECTION LIKE THIS... BLASTED LABOUR PARTY 30 ODD POINTS AHEAD IN THE POLLS AND LOOKING LIKE SURE-FIRE WINNERS... FRANKLY I'M NOT OPTIMISTIC ABOUT MY CHANCES...
I SPEND ALL MY TIME PHONING ROUND, VISITING PEOPLE, BUT THEY'RE NOT INTERESTED IN ANYTHING I'VE GOT TO SAY... HALF THE TIME THEY WON'T EVEN SPEAK TO ME...
YOU SHOULD GIVE UP, OLD CHAP...
IT'S A NIGHTMARE, JULIAN...WHEN ONE IS TRYING TO PERSUADE ONE'S CLIENTS TO DEAL THERE ARE NO WORSE MARKET CONDITIONS THAN TOTAL CERTAINTY...
...COME OUT CANVASSING WITH ME INSTEAD...GET AWAY FROM THAT DESK.

Alex
BEATTIE + TAYLOR
I'VE ALWAYS BEEN RUGBY MAD, ALEX, BUT I'M THINKING IT MIGHT BE SENSIBLE TO START CONCENTRATING ON PLAYING CRICKET NOW INSTEAD. WHAT DO YOU THINK?
AUSTIN! HOW OLD ARE YOU? ONLY 23!
YOUNGER GUYS LIKE YOU HAVE TO REMEMBER THAT CRICKET IS A FINE GAME WHEN YOU GET A BIT OLDER AND WANT TO SLOW DOWN... BUT AT YOUR AGE IT'S DIFFERENT...
YOU'RE YOUNG, YOU'RE ENERGETIC, YOU'RE STILL FIERCELY COMPETITIVE... YOU NEED TO EXPRESS ALL THAT THROUGH SOME FORM OF SERIOUS "CONTACT" SPORT...
YEAH, THAT'S ME ALL RIGHT...
email: alex-cartoon@etgate.co.uk
SO I SIGN UP FOR THE BANK'S CRICKET TEAM, RIGHT?
EXACTLY. ANY JUNIOR WORTH HIS SALT WANTS TO GET NETWORKING AND MAKING CONTACTS WITH SENIOR PERSONS DOESN'T HE?

RING RING

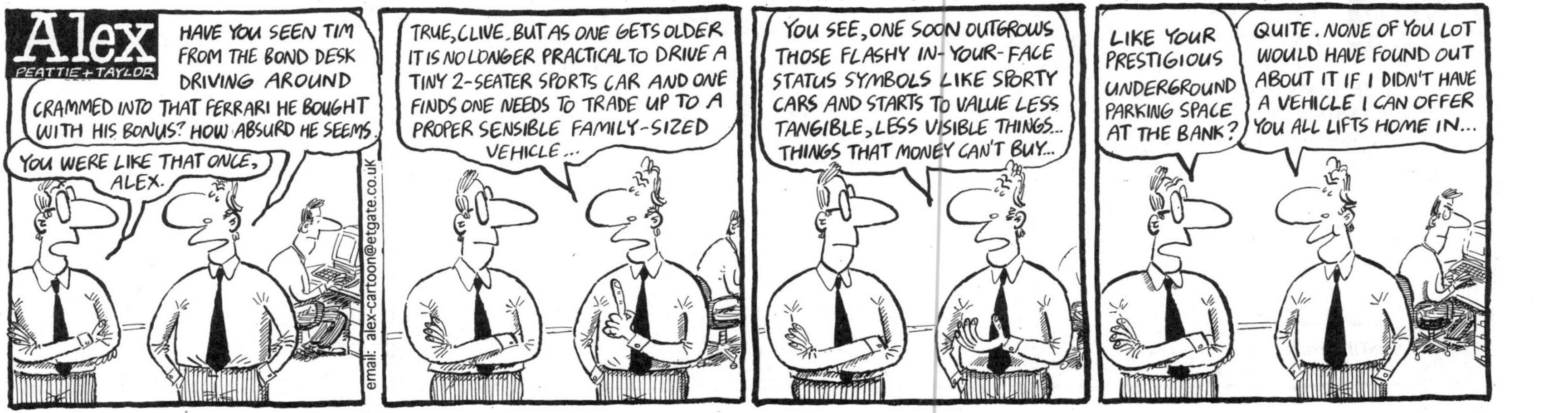
Alex
PEATTIE + TAYLOR
HAVE YOU SEEN TIM FROM THE BOND DESK DRIVING AROUND CRAMMED INTO THAT FERRARI HE BOUGHT WITH HIS BONUS? HOW ABSURD HE SEEMS.
YOU WERE LIKE THAT ONCE, ALEX.
email: alex-cartoon@etgate.co.uk
TRUE, CLIVE. BUT AS ONE GETS OLDER IT IS NO LONGER PRACTICAL TO DRIVE A TINY 2-SEATER SPORTS CAR AND ONE FINDS ONE NEEDS TO TRADE UP TO A PROPER SENSIBLE FAMILY-SIZED VEHICLE...
YOU SEE, ONE SOON OUTGROWS THOSE FLASHY IN-YOUR-FACE STATUS SYMBOLS LIKE SPORTY CARS AND STARTS TO VALUE LESS TANGIBLE, LESS VISIBLE THINGS... THINGS THAT MONEY CAN'T BUY...
LIKE YOUR PRESTIGIOUS UNDERGROUND PARKING SPACE AT THE BANK?
QUITE. NONE OF YOU LOT WOULD HAVE FOUND OUT ABOUT IT IF I DIDN'T HAVE A VEHICLE I CAN OFFER YOU ALL LIFTS HOME IN...

Alex
PEATTIE + TAYLOR
A LOT OF US MARKET MAKERS COMPLAIN THAT IN MOST INDUSTRIAL AND OTHER SECTORS ACTIVITY IS VERY SLUGGISH BECAUSE OF THE ELECTION...
YEAH... EVERYONE'S MINDS ARE ON OTHER THINGS...
BUT PERSONALLY I THINK IT'S GOOD TO SEE WE CAN STILL HAVE A LEVEL OF DEBATE ABOUT ISSUES IN THIS COUNTRY... EVEN IF IT IS TRUE THAT THE MARKETS ARE A BIT QUIET...
I MEAN TO BE HONEST I'M JUST SITTING AT MY DESK LIKE EVERYONE ELSE BUT I'M DOING SWEET F. A. BUSINESS...
ME TOO...
I'M DOING A ROARING TRADE WITH FOOTBALL CLUB FLOTATIONS... SWEET AS A NUT ISN'T IT?
IT'S THE ONLY THING PEOPLE WANT TO TALK ABOUT WHILE THE ELECTION'S MONOPOLISING THE NEWS...
F.A. CLUBS REPORT

Alex
PEATTIE + TAYLOR
I'VE TAKEN A MONTH OFF FROM METROBANK TO STAND AS A CONSERVATIVE CANDIDATE IN THE ELECTION, BUT IT'S A PRETTY GRIM STORY SO FAR...
PUB
I KNOW WHAT YOU MEAN. IT SEEMS ALMOST 100% CERTAIN THAT THE CONSERVATIVES WILL BE TOTALLY WIPED OUT WHEN THE COUNTRY GOES TO THE POLLS ON MAY 1ST...
WHATEVER PEOPLE SAY, THE PROSPECT OF A LABOUR GOVERNMENT SWEEPING TO POWER WITH A HUGE LANDSLIDE MAJORITY IS NOT GOOD NEWS FOR THE BUSINESS OF PEOPLE LIKE ME...
I HAVEN'T BEEN ABLE TO ENTICE A SINGLE ONE OF YOUR CLIENTS OUT TO LUNCH...
THEY'RE ALL CERTAIN YOU'LL LOSE YOUR DEPOSIT AND BE BACK AT YOUR DESK ON MAY 2ND...

Alex
PEATTIE + TAYLOR
JAMES! I KNOW YOUR BANK REIMBURSES ALL YOUR ENTERTAINING EXPENSES BUT I'VE FOUND THIS ITEM ON YOUR CREDIT CARD STATEMENT FOR THE AMSTERDAM TRIP YOU TOOK CLIENTS ON LAST MONTH...
EEK! THE "LAPS OF JUDGEMENT" GIRLIE BAR... YOU FOUND OUT...
I'M SORRY... I WAS WEAK... OKAY, I CONFESS :- LOOK I WENT WITH CLIENTS BUT WE HARDLY HAD ANYTHING TO DRINK ... NO-ONE HIRED ANY HOOKERS OR ANYTHING... I ONLY SAW ONE STRIPPER...
THE CLIENTS WANTED ME TO STAY FOR AN ALL NIGHT SESSION BUT I ONLY WENT IN FOR FIVE MINUTES AND ALL I HAD WAS ONE DRINK AND THEN I WENT BACK TO THE HOTEL... LOOK I'M SO SORRY...
I SEE...
YOU LAZY, LAZY B*ST**D... SO THAT'S WHY THIS IS THE LOWEST CLIENT HOSPITALITY BILL EVER... HOW ARE WE GOING TO COLLECT THE CREDIT CARD AIR MILES FOR A DECENT HOLIDAY LIKE THIS...?
I WAS EXAUSTED... I'LL STAY UP ALL NIGHT NEXT TIME... I PROMISE...

ZZZZ
DO NOT AROUSE

Alex
PEATTIE + TAYLOR
I HEAR BURTON ASKED FOR TIME OFF TO STAND FOR PARLIAMENT...
YES. NO CHANCE OF HIS GETTING IN OF COURSE... HE WANTS TO COME BACK ONCE THE ELECTION IS OVER...
...BUT IT SAYS A LOT ABOUT A CHAP OF HE'S PREPARED TO TAKE FOUR WEEKS OUT OF HIS LIFE TO GO AND DO SOMETHING LIKE THAT... IT'S MOST REASSURING IN THESE CYNICAL TIMES...
I'M GLAD TO HAVE A YOUNG MAN LIKE HIM WORKING AT THE BANK... WHAT HE'S TRYING TO DO SHOWS THAT HE'S STABLE, RESPONSIBLE, HAS INTEGRITY AND A REAL SENSE OF DUTY...
YES.
AND NOT SOME HUGE DODGY DERIVATIVES POSITION THAT WOULD ONLY GET FOUND OUT IF HE TOOK TIME OFF WORK...
QUITE. GOOD MAN. I TOLD HIM TO GET STUFFED; HE WAS TO STAY AT HIS DESK...

Alex
PEATTIE + TAYLOR
EVEN THOUGH CITY PEOPLE ARE FEELING PRETTY AFFLUENT AT THE MOMENT IT WOULD BE FOOLISH FOR CHARITY ORGANISERS TO GET TOO COMPLACENT.
AUCTION
IT'S ALL VERY WELL FOR GENEROUS BENEFACTORS LIKE OURSELVES TO POUR MONEY INTO A CHARITY'S COFFERS VIA AUCTIONS AND THE LIKE BUT THERE'S A REAL CONCERN ABOUT WHAT THAT MONEY IS SPENT ON...
YES INDEED.
AUCTION
THERE'S AN UNDERSTANDABLE WORRY AMONG US ABOUT OUR MONEY BEING WASTED, AS OPPOSED TO BEING USED TO PURCHASE USEFUL GOODS AND SERVICES...
THAT'S VERY TRUE...
...WHICH IS WHY NO-ONE BID FOR THE GOLD WRISTWATCH... IN CASE PEOPLE THOUGHT WE ACTUALLY WANTED IT.
QUITE... WHEREAS THE BIDDING FOR A MINI HELIUM BALLOON WITH THE CHARITY LOGO ON IT IS UP TO A MACHO £5000...

Alex
BEATTIE + TAYLOR
YOU KNOW, ALEX, MY NEW BOSS HAS AN "OPEN DOOR" POLICY FOR ALL EMPLOYEES.. HE DOESN'T EVEN HAVE A SECRETARY.
HE RECKONS A MODERN EXECUTIVE DOESN'T NEED ONE, WHAT WITH P.C.s, VOICE-MAIL, GSM MOBILE PHONES AND SO ON... PLUS IT FACILITATES COMMUNICATION WITH HIS SUBORDINATES...
YOU KNOW HOW IT IS IN MOST OFFICES - THERE'LL BE SOME BUSTLING INTERFERING P.A. WHO'LL PREVENT YOU FROM SEEING YOUR BOSS DIRECTLY AND INSIST THAT SHE BE THE CONDUIT FOR ALL DEALINGS WITH HIM...
WHICH IS JOLLY HANDY WHEN SUBMITTING ONE'S EXPENSES... DRAT!...
YOUR BILL, SIR
HMM... YES. ONE WOULDN'T WANT TO BE PHYSICALLY PRESENT TO BE QUIZZED BY THE BOSS WHEN HE'S SIGNING OFF THIS LOT...

EXPENSES CLAIM

Alex
PEATTIE + TAYLOR
SO YOU'VE GRANTED ROBIN BAKER TIME OFF TO CONTEST A SEAT FOR THE CONSERVATIVES IN THE ELECTION?
YES INDEED... ONLY A SLENDER CHANCE OF SUCCESS OBVIOUSLY...
..BUT WELL WORTH MAKING A GO OF, I FEEL... AND A SPECTACULAR COUP IF SOMEHOW IT COULD BE PULLED OFF... A LOT OF HYPOCRISY INVOLVED, PRETENDING TO HAVE OTHER PEOPLE'S INTERESTS AT HEART WHEN YOU'RE JUST OUT FOR YOURSELF..
email: alex-cartoon@etgate.co.uk
YOU KNOW, COMING OVER AS COMMITTED AND CARING WHEN THE WHOLE TIME YOU'RE LYING THROUGH YOUR TEETH AND TRYING TO WHEEDLE YOUR WAY OUT OF SPENDING COMMITMENTS.
QUITE... QUITE...
..BUT THAT'S HOW IT IS WITH "CONSTRUCTIVE DISMISSAL"... A SHAME THAT BAKER'S ALMOST CERTAIN TO LOSE...
SIGH YES, I SUPPOSE I'LL END UP JUST HAVING TO SACK HIM AND PAY HIM OFF...

Alex
PEATTIE + TAYLOR
Over the last few years the laptop computer has become a valuable addition to the executive's armoury...
TAP TAP
Apart from its use in meetings for calling up documents and note-taking it has also revolutionised the business world in its capacity for instantaneous transmission of information.
TAP
Computer-to-computer electronic messages can now be beamed across the ether over distances where direct and immediate communication would not previously have been imaginable.
TAP TAP
email: alex-cartoon@etgate.co.uk
.. like about 3 feet via the infra-red docking facility..
God, this meeting's dull. Have you noticed the client is wearing a polyester tie..?
TICK TICK
TAP
YAWN
TAP

Good morning Alex
Shhhh!
1ST CLASS

Alex
PEATTIE + TAYLOR
YOU KNOW WHAT THE INSPECTORS ARE LIKE ON THESE TRAINS. THEY TAKE AN OFFICIOUS SADISTIC PLEASURE IN PULLING UP PASSENGERS TRAVELLING WITHOUT A VALID TICKET...
1ST
THE PROBLEM IS, IT CAN BE HARD TO SPOT THEM WHEN THEY TURN UP IN PLAIN CLOTHES INSTEAD OF THE UNIFORM THAT WOULD FLAG THEIR IDENTITY TO THE REST OF THE CARRIAGE...
1ST
email: alex-cartoon@etgate.co.uk
THEY MAY LOOK JUST LIKE AN ORDINARY PASSENGER WEARING EVERYDAY CASUAL CLOTHES BUT THEY COULD TURN OUT TO BE SOMETHING ELSE...
1ST
IE. :- A GENUINE FIRST CLASS SEASON TICKET HOLDER... DAMN! I WAS LOOKING FORWARD TO HIM GETTING A FINE...
SO WAS THE INSPECTOR... BLASTED "DRESS-DOWN" FRIDAYS...
THANK YOU, SIR...
1ST

Alex
PEATTIE + TAYLOR
YOU TOOK A FRIEND OUT TO A BOOZY LUNCH AND BILLED IT TO THE BANK? HOW WILL YOU GET AWAY WITH IT?
OH, THERE'S A TRICK TO THAT...
I SIMPLY PHONE UP A TAME CLIENT AND ASK HIM MEANINGFULLY IF HE "ENJOYED LUNCH TODAY"... HE NOTES THE DATE IN HIS DIARY AND WILL BACK ME UP IF THERE'S ANY LATER QUERY OVER MY EXPENSES...
email: alex-cartoon@etgate.co.uk
SO DID THE CLIENT YOU PHONED GET THE HINT?
NOT EXACTLY. HE WAS INCOHERENT, ALMOST COMATOSE... HAD EVIDENTLY BEEN OUT AT A MASSIVE LUNCH HIMSELF...
GAVE ME A BIG ORDER THOUGH... HE MUST HAVE THOUGHT IT WAS WITH ME...

Alex
PEATTIE + TAYLOR
SO, RICHARD, HOW'S THAT SEAT YOU'RE CONTESTING FOR THE CONSERVATIVES?
NOT GOING WELL, ALEX. YOU DON'T KNOW WHAT IT'S LIKE CAMPAIGNING IN SOME DISTANT RURAL CONSTITUENCY...
FRANKLY I'M A CITY-DWELLER WHOSE EXPERTISE IS IN THE FINANCIAL MARKETS. NOW, OBVIOUSLY I'VE BONED UP ON ALL THE MAJOR NATIONAL POLITICAL ISSUES...
BUT I WASN'T PREPARED FOR THE NEGATIVE CAMPAIGNING - PUBLIC SLANGING MATCHES AND MUD-SLINGING... NOT TO MENTION ALL THE LOCAL RURAL ISSUES...
AH YES... I HEAR YOU HAD A PROBLEM OVER HEDGE ROWS...
IT GOT OUT THAT YOU'D HEDGED YOURSELF AGAINST LOSING BY "BUYING" LABOUR SEATS ON THE CITY INDEX SPREAD BETTING SERVICE...
AND THERE'VE BEEN SOME HUGE BLOODY ROWS ABOUT IT I CAN TELL YOU...

Alex
PEATTIE + TAYLOR
THE LAST FEW YEARS HAVE SEEN SOME REMARKABLE CHANGES IN EUROPE:- THE OPENING UP OF FRONTIERS, EX-COMMUNIST BLOC COUNTRIES COMING ON LINE...
email: alex-cartoon@etgate.co.uk
NATURALLY THERE'S BEEN A CORRESPONDING REVOLUTION IN COMMUNICATIONS. SUDDENLY WE'VE GOT THE INTERNET, E-MAIL, LAPTOP COMPUTERS AND MODEMS...NOT FORGETTING THESE NEW PAN-EUROPEAN GSM MOBILE PHONES.
ONCE THEY WOULD ONLY HAVE WORKED IN THEIR COUNTRY OF ORIGIN. NOW THEY CAN BE USED ALMOST ANYWHERE. IT'S GIVEN THE MODERN EUROPEAN BUSINESSMAN A NEW-FOUND POWER...
...TO EMBARRASS US IN PUBLIC WITH THEIR UNSEEMLY LOVE FOR THE BLASTED THINGS..
THIS COULDN'T HAVE HAPPENED 3 YEARS AGO. WILL SOMEONE PLEASE MAKE HIM SWITCH IT OFF...
Да..это я... я в лондоне
покупай

Alex
PEATTIE + TAYLOR
SO WHEN DID YOU START THINKING LABOUR WOULD WIN?
WHEN CERTAIN POLITICIANS STARTED EXTENDING THE HAND OF FRIENDSHIP TO THE BUSINESS COMMUNITY. I BELIEVE THAT WAS WHEN IT STARTED..
WHEN ONE SEES M.P.S OF A PARTY SUDDENLY STRIVING TO CEMENT GOOD RELATIONS WITH AND ESTABLISH A LEVEL OF CREDIBILITY WITH THE FINANCIAL WORLD ONE HAS TO TAKE NOTICE...
I SUPPOSE SO.
I MEAN THESE ARE PEOPLE WHO HAVE CLEARLY BECOME MUCH MORE PRAGMATIC AND FOCUSED ON THE PROSPECT OF WORKING WITH THE BANKING INSTITUTIONS AFTER THE ELECTION...
YES.
email: alex-cartoon@etgate.co.uk
YOU MEAN AS DIRECTORS AND CONSULTANTS ONCE THEY'RE KICKED OUT OF OFFICE?
QUITE. SEEING ALL THESE TORY M.P.S COMING IN AND GROVELLING FOR POST-MAY-IST JOBBIES YOU JUST KNOW THEY KNOW THEY'RE GOING TO LOSE...
THANKYOU FOR LUNCH RUPERT..
LET'S HAVE ANOTHER CHAT SOON..

NEWS
NEWS
LABOUR LAND-SLIDE
LIFT
TUG
LABOUR LANDSLIDE
LABOUR LANDSLIDE
LABOUR LANDSLIDE
LABOUR LANDSLIDE
LANDSLIDE
FLUMP

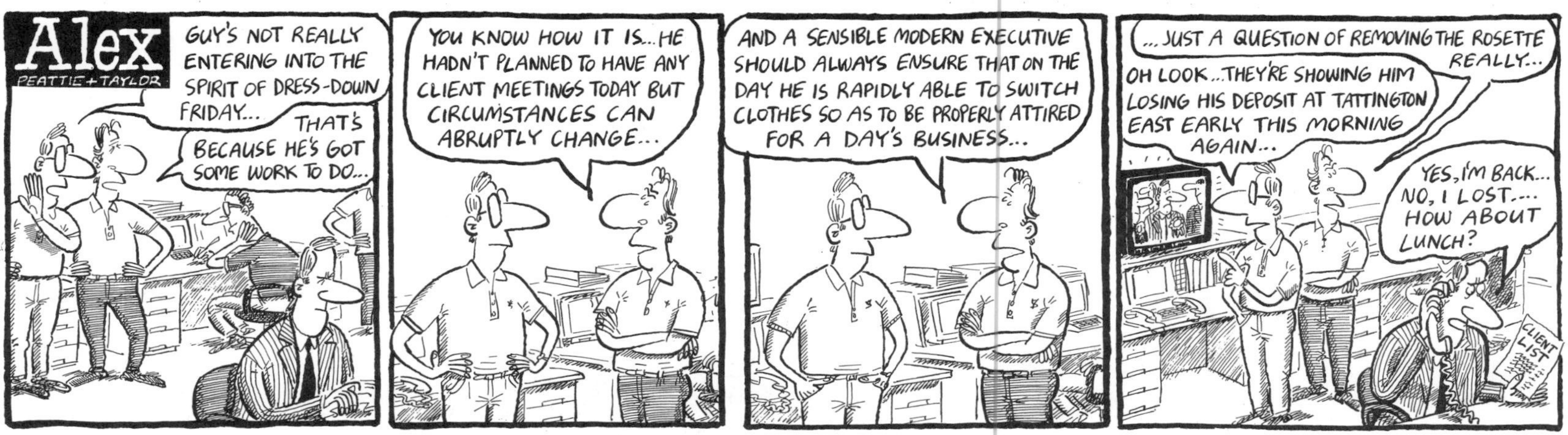
Alex
PEATTIE + TAYLOR
GUY'S NOT REALLY ENTERING INTO THE SPIRIT OF DRESS-DOWN FRIDAY...
THAT'S BECAUSE HE'S GOT SOME WORK TO DO...
YOU KNOW HOW IT IS... HE HADN'T PLANNED TO HAVE ANY CLIENT MEETINGS TODAY BUT CIRCUMSTANCES CAN ABRUPTLY CHANGE...
AND A SENSIBLE MODERN EXECUTIVE SHOULD ALWAYS ENSURE THAT ON THE DAY HE IS RAPIDLY ABLE TO SWITCH CLOTHES SO AS TO BE PROPERLY ATTIRED FOR A DAY'S BUSINESS...
... JUST A QUESTION OF REMOVING THE ROSETTE REALLY...
OH LOOK... THEY'RE SHOWING HIM LOSING HIS DEPOSIT AT TATTINGTON EAST EARLY THIS MORNING AGAIN...
YES, I'M BACK... NO, I LOST.... HOW ABOUT LUNCH?
CLIENT LIST

Alex
PEATTIE + TAYLOR
SORRY TO HEAR YOU DIDN'T MANAGE TO WIN THAT SEAT YOU CONTESTED AT THE ELECTION, GUY...
THANKS, ALEX. ACTUALLY I WAS JUST READING OVER THE SPEECH I WROTE FOR IF I GOT IN...
IT'S THE SORT OF GLORIOUS ORATION THAT ALL WE ASPIRING POLITICAL CANDIDATES FANTASISE ABOUT GIVING. YOU KNOW:- A CAPTIVE AUDIENCE AND ONESELF STANDING THERE ALL PROUD AND TRIUMPHANT...
ONE SPENDS SO MUCH TIME CRAFTING IT, REHEARSING IT, GETTING THE SENTIMENTS AND LANGUAGE RIGHT, FILLING IT FULL OF PASSION AND SINCERITY AND NOW IT'S JUST GOING TO END UP IN THE BIN...
COULD I READ IT FIRST?
SURE...
"... RIGHT, RUPERT, YOU OLD ♂✱@&, I'M GOING TO TELL YOU EXACTLY WHERE YOU CAN STICK YOUR JOB..."
AS IT WAS, I HAD TO GO TO HIM CAP IN HAND ON FRIDAY MORNING...

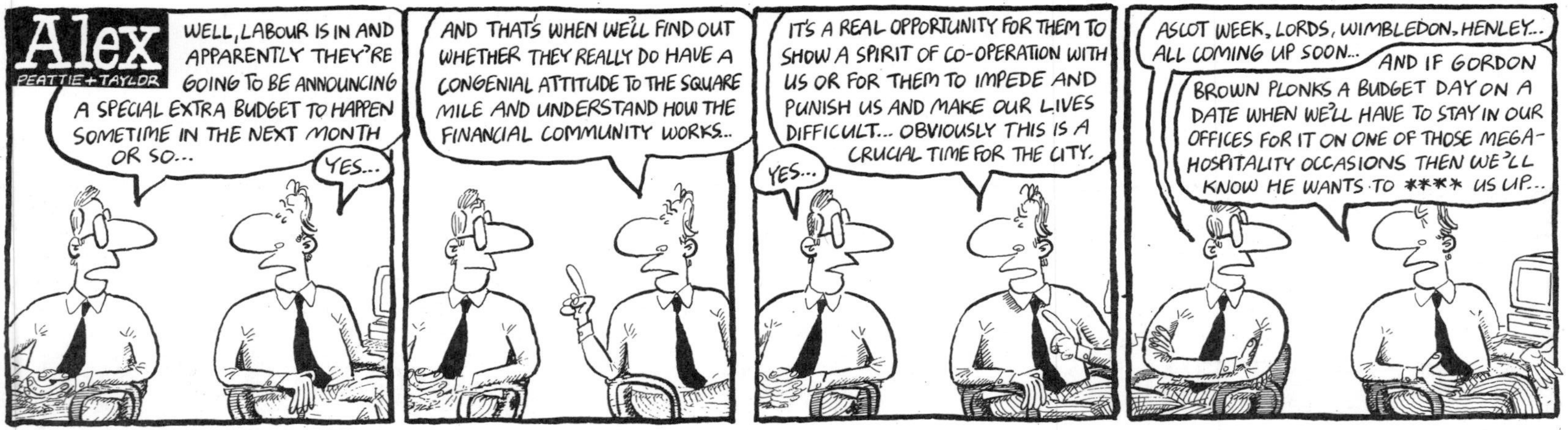
Alex
PEATTIE + TAYLOR
WELL, LABOUR IS IN AND APPARENTLY THEY'RE GOING TO BE ANNOUNCING A SPECIAL EXTRA BUDGET TO HAPPEN SOMETIME IN THE NEXT MONTH OR SO...
YES...
AND THAT'S WHEN WE'LL FIND OUT WHETHER THEY REALLY DO HAVE A CONGENIAL ATTITUDE TO THE SQUARE MILE AND UNDERSTAND HOW THE FINANCIAL COMMUNITY WORKS...
IT'S A REAL OPPORTUNITY FOR THEM TO SHOW A SPIRIT OF CO-OPERATION WITH US OR FOR THEM TO IMPEDE AND PUNISH US AND MAKE OUR LIVES DIFFICULT... OBVIOUSLY THIS IS A CRUCIAL TIME FOR THE CITY.
YES...
ASCOT WEEK, LORDS, WIMBLEDON, HENLEY... ALL COMING UP SOON...
AND IF GORDON BROWN PLONKS A BUDGET DAY ON A DATE WHEN WE'LL HAVE TO STAY IN OUR OFFICES FOR IT ON ONE OF THOSE MEGA-HOSPITALITY OCCASIONS THEN WE'LL KNOW HE WANTS TO **** US UP...

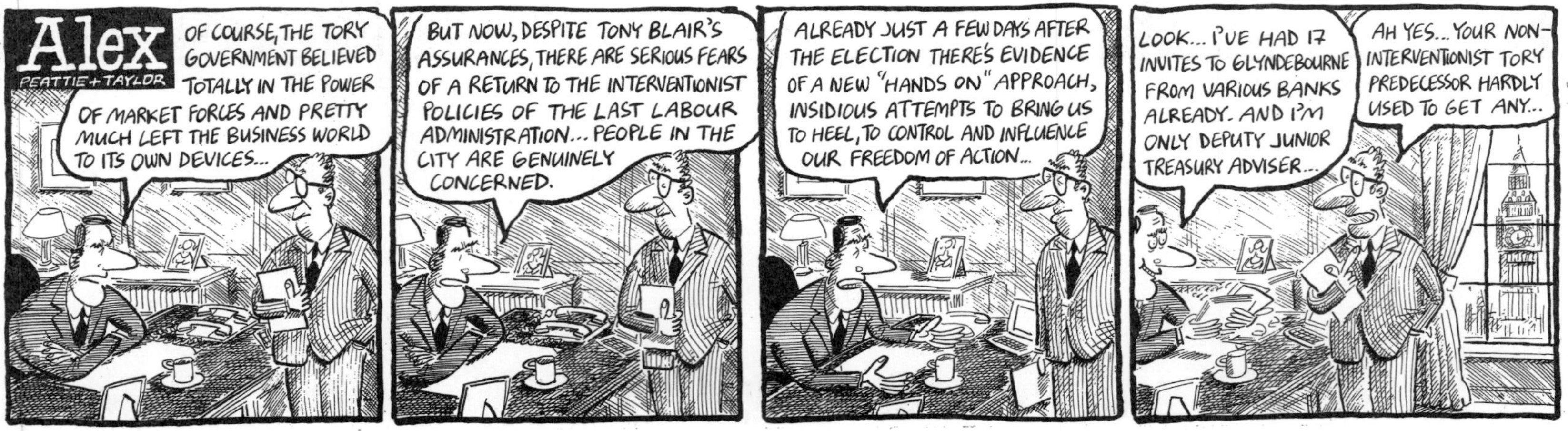
Alex
PEATTIE + TAYLOR
OF COURSE, THE TORY GOVERNMENT BELIEVED TOTALLY IN THE POWER OF MARKET FORCES AND PRETTY MUCH LEFT THE BUSINESS WORLD TO ITS OWN DEVICES...
BUT NOW, DESPITE TONY BLAIR'S ASSURANCES, THERE ARE SERIOUS FEARS OF A RETURN TO THE INTERVENTIONIST POLICIES OF THE LAST LABOUR ADMINISTRATION... PEOPLE IN THE CITY ARE GENUINELY CONCERNED.
ALREADY JUST A FEW DAYS AFTER THE ELECTION THERE'S EVIDENCE OF A NEW "HANDS ON" APPROACH, INSIDIOUS ATTEMPTS TO BRING US TO HEEL, TO CONTROL AND INFLUENCE OUR FREEDOM OF ACTION...
LOOK... I'VE HAD 17 INVITES TO GLYNDEBOURNE FROM VARIOUS BANKS ALREADY. AND I'M ONLY DEPUTY JUNIOR TREASURY ADVISER...
AH YES... YOUR NON-INTERVENTIONIST TORY PREDECESSOR HARDLY USED TO GET ANY...

Alex
PEATTIE + TAYLOR
WHAT DOES THE CITY THINK OF THE NEW LABOUR GOVERNMENT? WELL, WITH THE CONSERVATIVES WE KNEW WHERE WE WERE... THE FACES WERE FAMILIAR, THE POLICIES ESTABLISHED...
BUT NO-ONE KNOWS THE FIRST THING ABOUT THESE NEW MINISTERS, WHAT ARE THEIR REAL POLITICAL PERSUASIONS? AND WHAT INFLUENCES MAY BE BROUGHT TO BEAR ON THEM NOW THEY'RE IN OFFICE... THEY HAVE NO TRACK RECORD...
ALSO NO-ONE HAS ANY CLEAR IDEA OF WHAT LABOUR'S POLICY IS ON THE VITAL ISSUES: TAXATION, EUROPE, THE ECONOMY... ARE WE TO HAVE NEO-CONSERVATISM OR RADICAL SOCIALISM BY THE BACK DOOR? YOU CAN SEE WHAT THIS MEANS FOR US IN THE CITY....
PARADISE... WE CAN INVENT ANY NUMBER OF WILD FANCIFUL RUMOURS ABOUT LEAKED POLICY DOCUMENTS AND SPEECHES AND OUR CLIENTS WILL BELIEVE THEM...
CREATE A BIT OF VOLATILITY AND GET PEOPLE DEALING...

Alex
PEATTIE + TAYLOR
I'VE NEVER BEEN TO OUR OFF-SITE EMERGENCY PREMISES BEFORE...
ALL BANKS SET UP A FULLY-EQUIPPED DEALING ROOM IN CASE OF A DISASTER SUCH AS AN I.R.A. TERRORIST BOMB...
THOUGH WE'VE NEVER YET HAD OCCASION TO USE IT, IT'S GOOD TO KNOW IT'S HERE TO AID US IN THE UNDECLARED WAR AGAINST THOSE PEOPLE WHOSE SWORN MISSION IT IS TO SUBVERT AND DISRUPT THE RUNNING OF OUR BUSINESS...
THEY MAY THINK THEY'VE GOT THE WHAMMY ON US BUT THE EXISTENCE OF A FACILITY LIKE THIS HELPS US TO THWART AND FOIL THEM IN THEIR RUTHLESS INTENT...
THE PENPUSHERS IN THE "SERVICES SUPPORT" DEPARTMENT?
QUITE. WHEN THEY REFUSE US A REPLACEMENT SCREEN OR CHAIR FOR BUDGETARY REASONS WE JUST NICK ONE FROM HERE.
OOH. I FANCY A NEW WASTE PAPER BASKET...

Alex
PEATTIE + TAYLOR
AMAZING, ISN'T IT? NOT ONLY EVERY DEPARTMENT IN THE BUILDING, BUT EVERY ONE OF OUR OFFICES WORLDWIDE IS NOW LINKED BY OUR INTRANET AND E-MAIL FACILITY...
THESE DAYS EXECUTIVES CAN EXCHANGE INFORMATION VIA THEIR PCs GLOBALLY, INSTANTANEOUSLY, AT THE TOUCH OF A BUTTON...
JUST ANOTHER EXAMPLE OF MACHINES REPLACING PEOPLE IN THE MODERN TECHNOLOGICAL AGE, CLIVE.
WE ARE NO LONGER SO DEPENDENT ON A COMPLEX INFRASTRUCTURE OF P.A.s, MESSENGERS AND DRIVERS SCURRYING BACK AND FORTH... FRANKLY, E-MAIL HAS REPLACED THREE QUARTERS OF MY SECRETARY'S FUNCTION.
FURNISHING YOU WITH ALL THE LATEST OFFICE GOSSIP?
QUITE. NOW I CAN GET IT ALL OFF THIS THINGIE...
I STILL NEED HER TO SHOW ME HOW TO SWITCH IT ON THOUGH...

Alex
PEATTIE + TAYLOR
DRESS-DOWN FRIDAYS ARE SUCH A RELAXING OCCASION... BEING ABLE TO GET ON WITH ONE'S ROUTINE WORK WEARING ONE'S COMFORTABLE CLOTHES...
BUT I ALWAYS MAKE SURE I KEEP A SPARE SUIT IN THE OFFICE SO AS NOT TO GET CAUGHT OUT WHEN A QUICK CHANGE OF DRESS IS REQUIRED...
OF COURSE. ME TOO...
ONE SHOULDN'T FORGET THAT BANK PROTOCOL DEMANDS THAT ON ANY OCCASION WHEN ONE IS INTERFACING WITH CLIENTS ONE IS EXPECTED TO BE CORRECTLY ATTIRED IN ONE'S PINSTRIPE...
YES INDEED...
...CONSIDERING I INTEND TO PUT OUR IMPENDING 5-HOUR BINGE THROUGH AS A CLIENT LUNCH ON EXPENSES, BEST NOT TO BE SEEN DEPARTING IN ONE'S MUFTI...
LIFT
AH, ALEX, CLIVE... OFF TO LUNCH?
RECEPTION

Alex
PEATTIE + TAYLOR
SO WHAT DO YOU THINK OF THESE NEW EDUCATION PROPOSALS TO BAN CALCULATORS FOR CHILDREN UNDER 8?
SEEMS A VERY RADICAL MOVE...
DEPRIVING KIDS OF CALCULATORS WOULD ALMOST CERTAINLY REVEAL A SHOCKING LACK OF BASIC NUMERACY AMONG A GENERATION THAT HAS BECOME TOTALLY RELIANT ON ELECTRONIC AIDS...
I AGREE...
email: alex-cartoon@etaate.co.uk
FACED WITH HOMEWORK WHICH REQUIRES HIM TO WORK OUT SIMPLE SUMS IN HIS HEAD TODAY'S LAZY SEVEN-YEAR-OLD WILL INSTINCTIVELY TURN TO THE QUICK AND EASY METHOD OF ARRIVING AT THE ANSWER...
I.E. ASKING HIS DAD, WHO, EMBARRASSINGLY, ALSO WOULDN'T HAVE A CLUE WITHOUT A CALCULATOR...
HEM HEM... YES... WOULDN'T WANT THAT TO COME OUT ... WHICH IS WHY I SAY LET THE KIDS KEEP THE THINGS...

Alex
BEATTIE + TAYLOR
SO, RUPERT, PLEASED ABOUT THE IDEA OF SITTING ON A GOVERNMENT ADVISORY COMMITTEE?
OH YES. I WAS VERY EXCITED WHEN THE CALL CAME THROUGH FROM DOWNING STREET...
WITH LITTLE EXPERIENCE OF THE CITY, THE LABOUR PARTY NEEDS OUR INPUT IN IMPLEMENTING ITS POLICY OF MODERNISATION THAT'S ALREADY STARTED WITH SWEEPING REFORMS TO REGULATION AND THE BANK OF ENGLAND...
email: alex-cartoon@etgate.co.uk
WORKING WITH TONY BLAIR'S NEW-LOOK INFORMAL ADMINISTRATION WE WEAR LOUNGE SUITS INSTEAD OF BLACK TIE AT OFFICIAL FUNCTIONS AND PEOPLE GET TO BE CALLED BY THEIR FIRST NAMES...
YOU MEAN LIKE WHEN YOU BECOME "SIR RUPERT"?
EXACTLY. THAT'S ONE TRADITION THEY SIMPLY MUSTN'T TINKER WITH...
GETTING A GONG FOR IT IS THE WHOLE POINT...

Alex
PEATTIE + TAYLOR
2ND CLASS IS SO CROWDED TODAY... AND I KNOW FOR A FACT THERE ARE SEATS AVAILABLE IN 1ST CLASS...
2ND CLASS
YES... WE SHOULD JUST GO AND SIT THERE REALLY...
I MEAN: IS ONE ALLOWED TO JUST GO AND SIT IN ANOTHER CARRIAGE WHERE YOU'RE NOT REALLY ENTITLED TO BE BECAUSE YOU HAVEN'T BOUGHT THE RIGHT TICKET?
2ND CLASS
I SHOULDN'T THINK SO...
I'VE GOT A FEELING IT'S SOMETHING THE TICKET STAFF TRY TO DISCOURAGE WITH ON-THE-SPOT FINES THESE DAYS...
WHAT, SUMMARY ONES?
YES...
IT'S HARDLY AN ISSUE ON WINTERY DAYS IS IT...? US 1ST CLASS SEASON TICKET HOLDERS ONLY INFILTRATE THESE CARRIAGES WHEN THE TOTTY IS IN SKIMPY SUNWEAR...
COR! YOU DON'T GET BABES LIKE THAT IN 1ST CLASS DO YOU?

2ND CLASS
CITY + FINANCIAL
SUN

Alex
PEATTIE + TAYLOR
FRUIT JUICES AT LUNCHTIME? BUT YOU GUYS DRINK PINTS...
WITH OUR BOSS LIABLE TO POP IN HERE AT ANY TIME WE HAVE TO WATCH WHAT WE DRINK, CLIVE...
AND WHEN ALL THESE ANTI-BOOZING MEMOS ARE DOING THE ROUNDS BACK AT WORK... WELL, WE DON'T MIND CHANGING OUR HABITS A BIT IF IT'S COMPANY POLICY, DO WE, LADS?
NAH...
NAH...
email: alex-cartoon@etgate.co.uk
I MEAN WHEN YOUR EMPLOYERS IN THEIR WISDOM DECIDE THEY WANT TO SEE EMPLOYEES HAVE AN ORANGE JUICE AT LUNCHTIME YOU'VE GOT TO SHOW WILLING, RIGHT?
RIGHT.
WE CAN GIVE IT A SHOT AT LEAST...
YEAH.
WHAT OF? VODKA PRESUMABLY.
TEQUILLA ACTUALLY. I'VE HAD ELEVEN.
SLURP
WHOOPS

Alex
PEATTIE + TAYLOR
DID YOU KNOW THAT EMPLOYEES IN THE STATES WHO FEEL TRAUMATISED BY THEIR COMPANY'S CASUAL DRESS POLICY ARE PUTTING THE MATTER IN THE HANDS OF THEIR SOLICITORS?
AMAZING.
OF COURSE IT COULD NEVER HAPPEN OVER HERE. THOUGH MANY COMPANIES HAVE A DRESS-DOWN FRIDAY, IT'S PERFECTLY NORMAL TO KEEP A SET OF FORMAL BUSINESS CLOTHES IN THE OFFICE FOR CLIENT MEETINGS ETC.
FRANKLY IF I KNEW SOMEONE WHO FELT MILDLY UNHAPPY ABOUT HIS COMPANY'S POLICY OF ENCOURAGING PEOPLE TO COME INTO WORK IN CASUAL CLOTHES I'D SIMPLY ADVISE HIM TO BRING A SUIT...
EXACTLY RIGHT...
email: alex-cartoon@etgate.co.uk
SUE THE PANTS OFF HIS EMPLOYER FOR SARTORIAL HARASSMENT.... SADLY, ONE WOULD NEVER GET AWAY WITH IT IN THIS PATHETIC COUNTRY...
NOW IN THE STATES THEY'VE GOT A SENSIBLE MATURE ATTITUDE TO LITIGATION...
GRIFFIN & BROWN SOLICITORS AT LAW

Alex
PEATTIE + TAYLOR
APPARENTLY TONY BLAIR IS ABSOLUTELY FURIOUS ABOUT THE BOARDROOM OF CAMELOT AWARDING THEMSELVES HUGE DIRECTORS' SALARY INCREASES...
NEWS BLAIR ANGER AT LOTTO CHIEFS
IT'S A BIT CRASS, ISN'T IT?
YOU'D THINK, CONSIDERING THE NAME OF THEIR COMPANY, THAT BEFORE THEY BUMPED UP THEIR PAY THEY MIGHT HAVE BEEN MORE MINDFUL OF THE CHIVALRIC IDEALS FOR WHICH THE ORIGINAL CAMELOT WAS FORMED...
ER...
email: alex-cartoon@etgate.co.uk
WHAT, A BUNCH OF GUYS SITTING ROUND A TABLE DECIDING ON HOW BEST TO BE KNIGHTS?
YES.
I MEAN THEY'VE CERTAINLY BLOWN THEIR CHANCES OF GETTING A GONG OUT OF THIS ADMINISTRATION, HAVEN'T THEY?

Alex
PEATTIE + TAYLOR
THIS PASSENGER'S SON HAS BEEN RUNNING AROUND BEING A NUISANCE...I MERELY THREATENED TO TELL HIM OFF...
AH...CHIEF STEWARD...
I MUST COMPLAIN ABOUT THIS ATTEMPT TO ERODE PARENTAL AUTHORITY...AS THE BOY'S FATHER IT IS FOR ME ALONE TO DECIDE THE SORT OF TREATMENT THAT SHOULD BE METED OUT TO HIM...
I RESENT JUMPED-UP OFFICIALS LIKE THIS WOMAN HERE TAKING MATTERS INTO HER OWN HANDS AND THREATENING DAMAGING MEASURES WHICH WILL AFFECT MY FAMILY'S RELATIONSHIPS.
SIR, I MERELY SAID THAT IF YOUR SON CONTINUED TO MISBEHAVE I WOULD HAVE TO UPBRAID HIM...
OH... SORRY... I THOUGHT YOU SAID "UPGRADE" HIM... OH, DO WHAT YOU LIKE WITH THE BRAT AS LONG AS YOU KEEP HIM BACK THERE IN ECONOMY...
ER.. ANY CHANCE OF SOME MORE CHAMPAGNE?

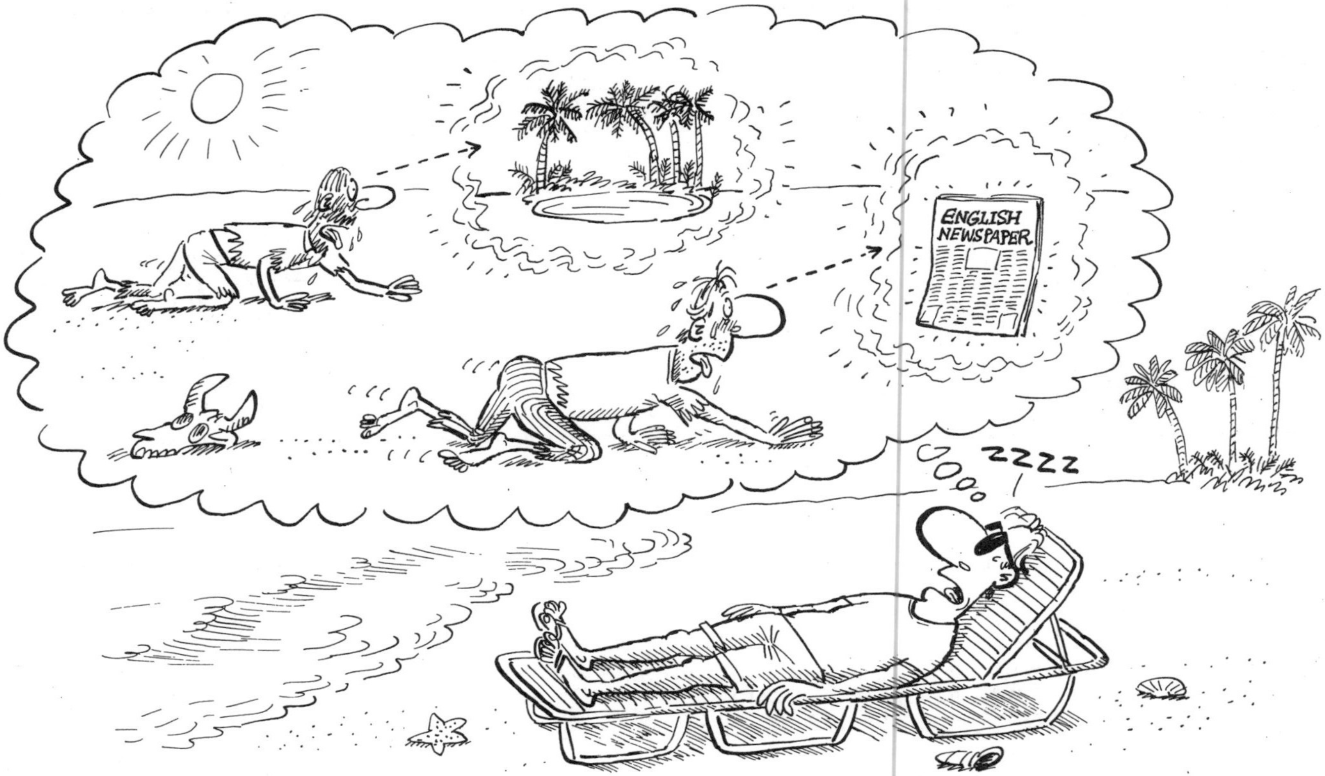
ENGLISH NEWSPAPER
ZZZZ

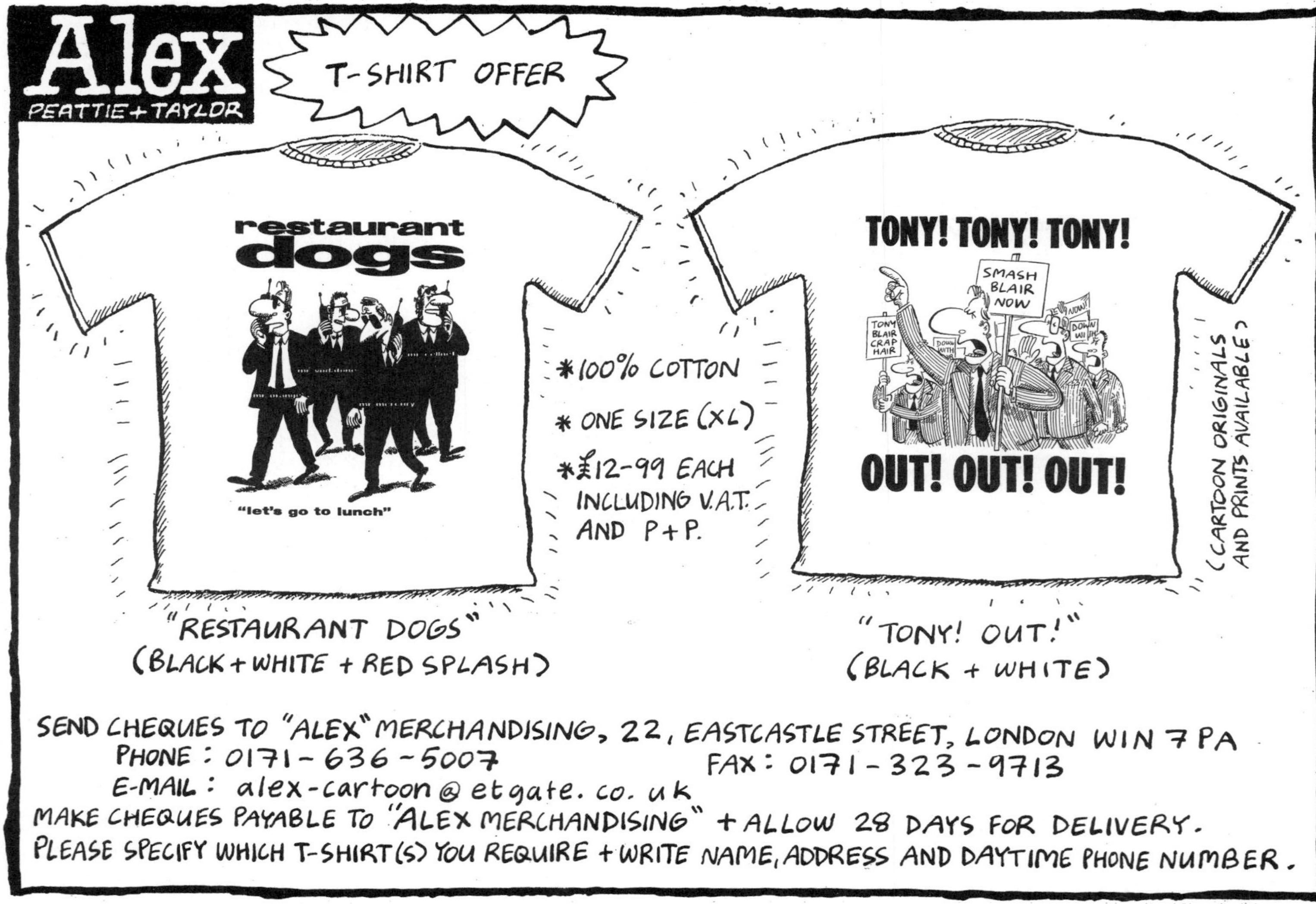

Alex
PEATTIE + TAYLOR
T-SHIRT OFFER
restaurant dogs
"let's go to lunch"
"RESTAURANT DOGS"
(BLACK + WHITE + RED SPLASH)
* 100% COTTON
* ONE SIZE (XL)
* £12-99 EACH INCLUDING V.A.T. AND P+P.
TONY! TONY! TONY!
SMASH BLAIR NOW
TONY BLAIR CRAP HAIR
OUT! OUT! OUT!
"TONY! OUT!"
(BLACK + WHITE)
(CARTOON ORIGINALS AND PRINTS AVAILABLE)
SEND CHEQUES TO "ALEX" MERCHANDISING, 22, EASTCASTLE STREET, LONDON W1N 7PA
PHONE: 0171-636-5007
FAX: 0171-323-9713
E-MAIL: alex-cartoon@etgate.co.uk
MAKE CHEQUES PAYABLE TO "ALEX MERCHANDISING" + ALLOW 28 DAYS FOR DELIVERY.
PLEASE SPECIFY WHICH T-SHIRT(S) YOU REQUIRE + WRITE NAME, ADDRESS AND DAYTIME PHONE NUMBER.